Unhinged
by Stacy Baker

Tate Publishing, LLC

"Unhinged" by Stacy Baker

Copyright © 2005 by Stacy Baker. All rights reserved.

Published in the United States of America
by Tate Publishing, LLC
127 East Trade Center Terrace
Mustang, OK 73064
(888) 361–9473

Book design copyright © 2005 by Tate Publishing, LLC. All rights reserved.

No part of this publication may be reproduced, stored in a retrieval system or transmitted in any way by any means, electronic, mechanical, photocopy, recording or otherwise without the prior permission of the author except as provided by USA copyright law.

Scripture quotations are taken from the Holy Bible, New International Version ®, Copyright © 1973, 1978, 1984 by International Bible Society. Used by permission of Zondervan Publishing House. All rights reserved.

All quotes, other than Scripture, are taken from the web site: http://www.brainyquote.com on 4–11–05 and 4–12–05.

This novel is a work of fiction. Names, descriptions, entities and most incidents included in the story are products of the author's imagination. Any resemblance to actual persons, events, and entities is entirely coincidental.

This book is designed to provide accurate and authoritative information with regard to the subject matter covered. This information is given with the understanding that neither the author nor Tate Publishing, LLC is engaged in rendering legal, professional advice. Since the details of your situation are fact dependent, you should additionally seek the services of a competent professional.

ISBN: 1–9332909–7-8

Cover design: Sommer Buss
Layout design: Kristen Polson
Cover model: Christy Tate
Hat for cover photo: Kathy's Treasure Chest, Mustang, OK
Gun for cover photo: Larry, Donna, and Joel Chumley.

Cover photo: Becky Picklo Photography specializes in photographing expectant mothers, newborn babies, children, and families. http://www.beckyphotography.com

Author photo used by permission. Lifetouch, Inc.

http://churchdirectories.lifetouch.com/contact.aspx

Dedication

Alan Baker

This book is dedicated to my love, my husband, Alan Baker.

Many years ago you stepped up to the plate and never looked back. You are a superhero in my eyes. You have worked so hard to take care of us, and you have met every need we ever had. You have wonderful parents who taught you to love the Lord and family passionately, and our children and I have reaped that love for many years, and those years have turned into our lifetimes. Above all, I love your faith and loyalty. As a disciple of Christ Jesus, as a husband, as a father, and as a friend, you have proven faithful and true. Your heart is brave, never wavering from what is righteous in God's eyes. Thank you for choosing us. I love you.

Luke Baker

Son, my prayer for you is that you will achieve your heart's desire—to make the name of God famous throughout all of the earth. God's eyes and heart are better than mine, and I know He keeps you. No matter where your call takes you, you are as close to my heart as the moment I first felt your heart beating next to mine.

I am proud of you, and I love you.

David Baker

Son, my prayer for you is that you will always continue to lead your family in the ways of the Lord, passing down a godly legacy to your children and grandchildren.

God made me a specific promise that He would take care of you, just as He did Joshua. You are a husband and a father now, but I will always hold you in my heart, just as I did when I carried you inside of me.

I am proud of you, and I love you.

Erin Baker

My prayer for you is that you will know what a special plan God has for your life. You are loved and appreciated. If I could handpick a daughter, I would pick you.

Your heart and spirit amaze me. You are a wonderful wife to our son and a great mother to our grandchildren. As you take time in a busy day to teach the girls to sing *Jesus Loves Me,* I know there is no sweeter sound being lifted to the Lord.

I am proud of you, and I love you.

Asley Baker

My prayer for you, Asley, is that you will be a great woman of God. I pray you will love the Lord with all of your heart. I know God has a special plan for your life.

You are such a joy to PaPa and to GiGi. I can see everything good in your dad and mom all wrapped up and packaged in you. You are so tenderhearted, and you love to sing songs to Jesus. I know Jesus loves to listen to your sweet, sweet voice.

I am proud of you, and I love you.

Braelyn Baker

My prayer for you, Braelyn, is that you will be a great woman of God. I pray you will love the Lord with all of your heart. I know God has a special plan for your life. PaPa and GiGi were given a second joy when you came into our lives. You are still tiny now, but I can see your sweet spirit. You are already being taught to praise God, and I know Jesus can't wait for you to say his name.

I am proud of you, and I love you.

Acknowledgments

Thank you to the Tate family...
If ever there was a family that had the ability and willingness to make dreams come true, it is the Tate family.

Thank you to Tate Publishing...
Nothing can be accomplished without teamwork. Such is the case with this book. Every one of you at Tate Publishing knows how special you are to me, and I love you all.

Thank you to the Fisher family...
Dan, you told me to write what I was passionate about, and I did. Your spiritual leadership changed my family's legacy and my life forever. Pam, you are one of my favorite chicks! Dan, Pam, Jacob, and Rebekah—I love you!

Thank you to the Davis family...
Gary and Belinda, you are like family. Thank you for your constant encouragement and love. Gary, Belinda, Kevin, Ginger, and Keith—I love you!

Thank you to my mother, Barbara Head...
If ever a mother made a daughter believe she could succeed, you did. You have poured your life into our family, and I love you.

My love to Alison, Kyle, and Jeanie Dill...
God promises that He has a special plan for each of you. I know that through Christ you will succeed because that is God's promise and He is faithful.

Thank you to the Baker family...
I can't imagine anything other than being part of your family. I am proud to have your name. I love each and every one of you.

With love to my church family at Trinity in Yukon, OK...
Dionne Forrest, I'm glad we met. Thanks for lending me *On Writing*.

A special thanks to the Costilows and the Ryans, for you held my hand from the very beginning so many, many years ago.

*How far you go in life
depends on your being
tender with the young,
compassionate with the aged,
sympathetic with the striving and
tolerant of the weak and strong.
Because someday in your life
you will have been all of these.*

GEORGE WASHINGTON CARVER

1

Jingle Bells played throughout the mall, blending in with the other Christmas noises. "Mommy, can we go see Santa Clause?" The little boy kept tugging on his mother's sleeve. With her arms full, she kept walking in a determined way to her next destination. The muffled sound of the bell ringer clanging his heavy bell drifted into the crisp air and floated into the department stores.

Noelle looked around the coffee bar as she sat and had a steaming cup of coffee. Christmastime was her favorite time of the year. Everyone rushed around, but the excitement and anticipation in the air made it seem okay. It made crazy seem right.

She really hadn't started her shopping yet, and time was running out. Noelle had to get serious, and she would—later.

The party tonight would be the event of the year. She thought about her dress. Occasions like this didn't happen very often, and she would be dressed to the nines.

Tonight everyone else would probably be dressed in black or red, denoting the holiday festivities. Not Noelle. The emerald green dress she had chosen matched her eyes and made them snap when they crinkled, and her dark complexion made her brilliant smile beam when she laughed.

There was only one thing missing in her seemingly perfect life.

● ● ●

She put on her favorite diamond earrings and took one last look in the mirror. While she could see her flaws, she had camouflaged them well. She looked like the million bucks that she dreamed of.

Noelle had a lot going for her, and tonight could be a big night. She was the editor of a major publishing house, and "meet and greets" were important. One of the authors invited to "Christmas at The Westminster" had not re-signed with his current publisher. Signing him to her company would be a significant accomplishment in her career. It would move her up on the publishing ladder and secure her position within her company.

Since her potential client was a published

author, he already had time to be labeled with the reputation of "difficult." Quite a few authors were difficult in all actuality so maybe he wouldn't be so bad. Creative people seemed to have a very eccentric way about them when it came to their work. Getting their work published was like letting go of a child, and they did it hesitantly.

The elevator took her from the penthouse to the lobby; she was greeted by the doorman who escorted her to the waiting limo. As he wished her a wonderful evening, she nodded in acknowledgment, but her mind was racing elsewhere.

Noelle had courted this man from the moment his last book was published. She tried to woo him and lure him shamelessly, but it was to no avail. He just blew her off. Not a word, not a response.

Yes, John Brittingham was a case all right—a head case. Several successful novels ago he made up his mind to look the part of the dashing and debonair bachelor. He was successful at that too. His signature? Fast cars and faster women. How would she break through to him? To persuade him to switch houses, she would have to meet his need. He didn't *need* a thing.

● ● ●

The limo neared The Westminster. The driver

kept the car in line as the other limos emptied their stunning clientele. She was next.

Many of the guests would show up with dates or spouses. That scenario was not part of Noelle's plan. The car rolled to a slow stop. She sat still as the chauffeur came around and opened her door. This was the first time she had stepped out onto an actual red carpet. Cameras flashed and reporters rushed her. The questions kept coming.

"Are you here to sign John Brittingham?"

"Why do you think he should switch houses? Are you going to publish his next movie script?"

So much for flying in under the wire. The truth? No one knew her. They only knew her publishing house. In addition, no one even really cared about the house, only John Brittingham. He was the cause of all this drama. If John spoke, people listened. If John wrote, people bought it. If John changed publishers, people took notice.

Noelle had her most sincere "No comment" down pat. The press moved on to the next limo with someone more exciting and titillating.

As she entered The Westminster, she was given a pass. This was an "Invitation Only" affair, and she was here by default. Her senior editor was out of town signing an author in South Africa. Truthfully, if he had thought the house stood a chance, he would have canceled his trip and flown in to do this himself.

His absence measured the amount of confidence he had in this merger. That was okay with Noelle; she believed. She didn't know what this guy, John, would be like, but she knew if she aimed for less than success that she would hit it. Tonight would be her night.

After receiving her pass, she started making her rounds. She had been in the industry for quite some time and knew lots of faces, if not all the names. As she worked the room, time seemed to be ticking away. She had seen no sign of John Brittingham. While these other contacts were important, they were not the target trophy.

She excused herself to the ladies' room and regrouped. When she reentered the room, she focused more pointedly on finding Mr. Brittingham. He seemed to be an illusive creature.

When she stepped back into the party, Santa had arrived. He had entered on a motorized sleigh and had gifts for every guest—passes to The Westminster's spa, fancy Westminster stationary, rounds of golf on The Westminster's golf course, and gift certificates to The Westminster Restaurant and The Westminster Gift Shoppe. These were all people who would not be doing without anything this Christmas, but they acted like small children as Santa lavishly covered them with gifts from his bottomless bag. This was PR at its best. You could bet these people would tell of their enchanted Christmas night at The

Westminster for years to come. The Westminster was legendary.

As the commotion continued, Noelle circled the perimeter of the room. Surely he hadn't slipped in and out without any notice from anyone. That was definitely not his preferred MO. He lived for the flashy, the exaggerated, and the beautiful.

He didn't let her down. There he was. He was taller than most of the other men in the room. While the tux he had on was a perfect fit, it seemed to play upon his features. He didn't look difficult; he looked boyishly charming.

The only thing standing between him and Noelle was about 450 other people wanting to talk to him too.

● ● ●

Noelle worked her way across the room, only stopping for pleasantries when absolutely necessary. The clock was still ticking. This might be her only chance to sign him on her own, while her boss was out of town. Imagine what a surprise it would be if she pulled this off. Imagine . . .

"Hello, Noelle."

"Oh, hi, Chris."

"What are you up to these days?"

"I'm still working for The Queen's House Publishing. What about you?"

"I'm still writing for my show. Are you guys here to try and sign John Brittingham?"

"*Us guys* aren't here. Roger is out of town so I'm filling in. As far as John Brittingham goes, of course we would like to sign him. So would half the people in this room."

"I've been trying to get some of his screen writing work. No luck so far."

"Sorry. Hey listen, I've got to go. Will you excuse me?"

Noelle pressed on. She really didn't know how stunning she looked. Heads turned as she cut through the center of the room this time. She commanded a powerful audience, and she got one.

John kept speaking to a captivated group of peers and associates as Noelle approached. While never breaking stride in his speech, his eyes locked onto the green gems looking back at him.

His attention did not go unnoticed by Noelle. She felt confident as she headed directly for him.

"Good to see you, Noelle."

"It's nice to see you too, Wilson." Noelle liked Wilson, but bumping into him now could not have happened at a worse time. Wilson was an author that had published three books through them already. None of the books were best sellers, but they were good books, and he had potential.

"Are you having a good time, Noelle?"

"Sure. Is your wife here with you, Wilson?"

"Yes. She ran into an old friend from college. They have a lot to catch up on. I'm just trying to meet new people and get my feet wet. I haven't had much experience at things like this yet. Any pointers?"

"Don't get any ideas about switching publishers!"

"No worries."

"Have a good time, Wilson. See you when you come in next week. Tell your wife 'hi' for me."

"Will do. See you later." Noelle escaped that in short.

Back to her plan . . . she glanced up. She had lost her focus on Brittingham. There was a crowd, but he was no longer visible. *Where could he have gone?* she asked herself. Her eyes darted quickly around the room. It was urgent that she find him.

She started walking the room, strategically trying not to get caught up with anyone in particular. He was nowhere to be found.

She stepped out onto the balcony. No such luck. He had vanished. Discouragement crept into the very center of her bones.

● ● ●

She collapsed down on her sofa and pulled off her earrings and necklace. Her feet were killing her. And for what? What a waste of time! This dress had cost a fortune, and she was already living above her means.

Not only that, but she had not used the opportunity to make any other connections. She had been sure that she could pull this off. Roger, her senior editor, would not be happy with her. She had nothing but sore feet and a high credit card bill to show for this evening.

As she got into bed, Noelle's mind raced. There still had to be a way. Roger wasn't due in for nine more days. This would be the most challenging nine days of her life. It was now or never.

Never give up,
for that is just the place
and time that the tide will turn.

HARRIET BEECHER STOWE

2

When she awoke the next morning, the clock said 8:45. Great! She was late! She twisted her hair and clamped it into place with a rhinestone clip. Her sweater with the fur collar had just come back from the cleaners, and it would look sharp with her black dress pants. She could put her make-up on in the taxi. Noelle finished up and dashed out the door. She had no choice but to call the office to let her assistant know what was going on.

"Noelle Reynolds' office."

"Jacqui, hi. It's me. I'm running late. Are they there yet?"

"They just got here. How late are you going to be?"

"I'm leaving my apartment now. I'd say 30 minutes or so. I'll hurry just as fast as I can."

"I'll stall—coffee and donuts. I can let them look at the reports until you get here. Will that work?"

"That would be great. Tell them I'm caught in traffic." She hoped that would not turn out to be true.

Jacqui was a great assistant. She was personable and always stayed a step ahead. She would be able to handle herself even if she didn't receive a warm reception when she told the Board about the delay.

Noelle hated feeling rushed and rattled. With Roger gone, this meeting was her responsibility. Just like last night, she had blown it. He would never trust her again. She had to get it together.

As she walked into her office, Jacqui filled her in on the status of the meeting. "Everyone is seated. Your files are laid out in presentation order. I told them you were delayed in traffic. They are restless but okay for the most part. They'll get over it."

"They'll get over it if they like my answers today. They are definitely a fickle lot, Jacqui. We'll just see what happens."

She knew she had to act confident, even if she wanted to run the other way. Noelle swung the door open and marched in with an assertive, "Good morning, everyone."

"Good morning," mumbled various members of the Board.

"Gentlemen, I apologize for my tardiness. It couldn't be helped. Let's get to the business at hand. We are here to discuss our bottom-line figures. Since Roger is out of town, he has asked me to step in for him."

Noelle Reynolds was nervous, but she kept it well hidden. These men were like animals. If she showed fear, they would eat her alive.

"Ms. Reynolds, we have some concerns," stated Mr. Devon, the senior member of the Board.

Noelle had learned long ago that the less she talked, the better off she would be. She didn't want to volunteer any information without just cause. She knew what their "concerns" were, but she wanted to deal with them on a priority basis.

"What are your specific concerns, gentlemen?"

"Our main concern is lost revenue. Our books are just not turning the kind of profit we were expecting."

"I assume you have thought about a solution for this dilemma."

"We haven't just *thought* about it. We've studied it."

"And what does your study reveal?"

"Besides watching our spending, we have two choices. We must turn another signed author of ours into a major success, or we must sign a well-known author."

"Which of our authors did you have in mind?"

"That's not the decision we have made, although we want to continue working toward that result. I'm sure you are well aware that John Brittingham has not re-signed with his publishing house. The word around industry circles is that he is not happy with the royalty fees they are offering him. We want him. We want you to make it happen."

"I see."

Noelle looked at the suits all sitting in a row. She wondered if they ever woke up late. Could they all pay their credit card bills? Did their shoes ever hurt their feet? Did they ever fail at anything?

"Gentlemen, what is your plan for making this happen?"

"Ms. Reynolds, we will leave that to you. If you signed him today, it would take another six months to get his next book out and on the shelf. The sooner you can make that happen, the better."

"I understand. I'll start working on him immediately."

As the meeting concluded, Noelle wondered if they were aware of how many times she had already tried to sign John Brittingham. She hadn't even been able to meet with him. This did not look good.

● ● ●

John Brittingham needed a shower. His run this morning lasted a little longer than normal. It felt good, but it was time to get things rolling.

He had to write at least 2000 words today. It was the daily goal he had set many years ago, and he stuck to it . . . usually. It had served him well over the years, and John felt almost religious about it. Success hadn't come easily, and he always felt under the gun to make it last.

His office didn't have any windows, but it was cozy. He felt at home there. There was no phone to distract him—only his computer beckoning him to a habitual, morning rendezvous. She coaxed him, even seduced him, to spend time with her. He didn't disappoint her; he was faithful to her. Everyday he was as equally hungry for her as the day before. Today was no different.

He assumed his familiar position behind his desk. The book was going well, and John had really been on a roll.

He typed, "Too many days had passed since he had seen her . . ." Then he stopped.

The woman in the green dress kept invading his thoughts. Those eyes haunted him—they taunted him. Who was she? Maybe he had misunderstood the look they shared last night. Maybe he had fabricated the entire "moment" in his mind, just as he fabricated all these other stories.

She had stopped to talk to another man and seemed in no hurry to meet him. He had probably made a fool of himself. Still, there was something different about that woman.

He cleared his mind; the regular woman in his life wouldn't wait, and she nudged him on. He began to type ...

● ● ●

Jacqui felt sorry for Noelle. She seemed to be getting in over her head. Jacqui had done everything she could to help her. Noelle was great to work for, and she would hate to have a different boss.

At the close of the meeting, Noelle walked the members out toward the elevators. Jacqui was anxious to talk to her when she stepped back inside.

"Hey, Noelle. How did it go last night?"

"Don't ask. I don't even want to talk about it. Let's just say it didn't 'go' at all."

"Are you going to keep trying to sign him?"

"I don't have any choice. The Board didn't give me an option. I'm afraid they are going to be disappointed."

"That's not true. If anyone can pull this off, you can. You just have to keep thinking. Where can you *accidentally* bump into him?"

"I don't know. I'm tired of thinking about it. I'm going into my office. Should John Brittingham call and ask to sign with us, buzz me. If not, hold all my calls."

"Done."

"Thanks, Jacqui. You're great."

"I *am* great now that I think about it." That finally drew a small grin from Noelle.

As Noelle closed the door to her office, she relived last night. John Brittingham was even better looking in person than he was on the jacket of his book. No wonder the women couldn't leave him alone. He looked like the leading character in every romance novel she had ever read. *Enough!* she told herself. This was not getting her any closer to his signature on a big, fat contract.

She picked up the phone and called his office. As usual, the machine came on saying that Mr. Brittingham was unavailable at the moment, but it offered the opportunity to leave a message—again.

She hung up. It was futile.

Noelle had always been creative. In school, her favorite class was drama. She loved the days when the teacher would have them work on improvisations. The skills it took to think on her feet then, served her well now.

She buzzed for Jacqui. "Jacqui, would you come in here, please?"

"Sure."

The door opened almost immediately. "Yes?"

"I want you to find a private investigator for me. Get me three or four to choose from. Set the interview appointments for today. The sooner, the better."

"May I ask why?"

"I'm out of time with our Mr. Brittingham. I know this seems drastic, but I am desperate. Please don't let them know why I need their services yet. I don't want this to get around town."

"I understand. I'll get on it right now."

Noelle was already second-guessing her own decision.

● ● ●

The interviews with the private investigators were fairly uneventful. One did stand out just because of an odd quirk he had. He kept clicking his ring on the arm of the chair while they talked. It struck Noelle that he acted nervous and distracted—almost seedy. Although he was a man in his late fifties, he didn't seem very grandfatherly for some reason. He appeared more like an uncle who always hung out at the racetrack and then bummed money off his brother-in-law.

Out of the four interviews, only one had potential. Her name was Molly Red, yet her name didn't match her look. Molly looked like she could be a soccer mom or a doctor. She had the kind of look that was adaptable, and it suited her lifestyle. Molly had only been a PI for three years, but she had handled some very high-profile cases.

After sizing her up, Noelle decided Molly would do just fine. She could blend in with all the other women who followed John around, and she could swoon when it was appropriate.

"I need someone immediately, Ms. Red."

"Please call me Molly. I am available today, Ms. Reynolds."

"Noelle," she corrected her. "That would be great. What do you need? Financially, I mean."

"$1200.00 up front. $500.00 a day, starting today. Time is measured in one-day increments. After midnight, you're in another day."

"Wow!" Noelle was a little dazed at the figures.

"The clock's running, Ms. Reynolds. Do we have a deal?"

"Deal," she answered decisively. "What else?"

"These are the rules. I won't do anything that will get me thrown in jail or anything that will give me a disease. At the price I charge, I understand the stakes are high. You're not just hunting a lost love or that old friend from high school, are you Noelle?" Noelle's eyes shifted downward as she glanced at the floor. "Didn't think so. Who is it?"

"Can you absolutely assure me this is confidential?"

"My reputation is squeaky clean. I have one other woman who works for me. It won't go further than the two of us."

"All right. We are trying to sign an author from a different publishing house. He is in limbo and hasn't re-signed his contract yet. I have nine days, including today, to get him signed. If not, I will probably lose my job."

"I understand. Who's the author?"

Noelle paused for moment before she spoke. "John Brittingham."

"I see."

"Do you think you can get to him?"

"I can get to anyone. What do you need me to do?"

"I have to find out his schedule—any special places he goes or any other available access where I will have the opportunity to speak with him privately. If I can talk to him, I think I can sign him. What do you think?"

"Give me three days. I'll have his basic schedule."

"Good luck. I've been trying for the last three months."

As Molly Red left her office, Noelle Reynolds had the urge to feel hopeful.

● ● ●

Although the book had been going great so far, John had been trying to finish Chapter 6 for two days. He just couldn't come up with the right ending. He pushed his chair back and stretched his legs out. As he stared at the ceiling, his mind began to wander.

It had been quite awhile since he had been in a long-term relationship. Meeting someone new was difficult. With his fame came distrust. He never knew if a woman liked him for himself. It always became a tangled mess.

John loved women. All women. He loved tall ones, short ones, dark ones, light ones, thin ones, and the ones who weren't so thin. He liked the way they smelled, the way their hair fell upon their shoulders, and the way they tilted their heads when they flirted with him.

Still, sometimes it got old. His parents had passed away four years ago in a car accident when a drunk driver hit them. He had no brothers or sisters. A distant aunt and uncle in Arizona remained as his only living relatives.

Christmastime was lonely by himself. Oh, he had a desk piled high with invitations to holiday events, but when he awoke on Christmas morning, he would be alone. The next two weeks would be long.

He stood up and went into the kitchen for a cup

of hot coffee. His kitchen was beautiful. Everything was stainless steel. Normally it seemed contemporary and sleek; today it had a somewhat cold feel to it.

As he leaned against the hard countertop, he gazed out of the big bay window and noticed that snow had started to fall. It was quiet in the country, and the snow bowed to the quietness. It whispered down as if to say, "Shhh. This is our secret."

He kind of wished he had put up a Christmas tree this year.

● ● ●

It had started snowing, but Noelle had to go shopping. Truthfully, she liked the snow. She liked how the streets were a little emptier, and the stores slowed down for just a moment. The city looked like it had put on a clean, new dress for Christmas. She bundled up tightly and left her office for the afternoon.

She had to get something for Jacqui. It needed to be something special. She was very dear to Noelle, not only as an assistant, but also as a friend. She still needed to buy something for her sister's family too. The twins were easy to buy for. If the toy had wheels or a trigger, the boys would like it.

The taxi pulled up, and she gladly climbed into the warmth. As she headed to the toy store, she kept thinking about her task ahead with John Brittingham. She had to stop thinking about it all the time. Christmas came but once a year.

As she searched for the right gift, her cell phone rang. "Noelle?"

"Yes, Jacqui?"

"Roger called. He wondered if you would be back in the office this afternoon. He wants to run some ideas by you."

"I really hadn't planned on it since I worked so late last night."

"I'll let him know. He said it might be tomorrow morning before he can call you back, anyway."

"Thanks, Jacqui." Noelle felt relief sweep over her. She needed a little more time before she discussed things with Roger.

She wondered what Molly had up her sleeve.

● ● ●

Molly found John's address within a matter of minutes. Next she made a map to his home from her laptop. It was a bit of a distance, almost 25 miles out in the country.

As she drove back to her office, she was curious about what this guy had that made him such a prize. Following him would be difficult if he lived in a secluded area, which was a high probability. She might need Stella's help with this case.

Stella Stone was blonde and simply irresistible

when it came to men. Men couldn't take their eyes off her. When she spoke, her voice was deep and throaty, and her audience was always captive.

She would be a great match for John Brittingham. He had a reputation for being a ... well, he had a reputation. If he met Stella, he would be interested in her.

Molly couldn't really assure Noelle of John's schedule in only a few days. That promise wasn't exactly the truth, but it was close. She *would* be able to get Noelle the access to him that she needed within three days. Molly was going to *create* a schedule for John; he just didn't know it yet. When he met Stella, any plans he had would be changing.

That was a promise Molly could keep.

*It is a terrible thing to see
and have no vision.*

HELEN KELLER

3

Stella Stone ground out her cigarette butt in the already too full ashtray. It had been a long time since she had given any serious thought to quitting her habit. It had become her friend, the deadly kind.

She needed money. Lots of money. Cigarettes weren't Stella's only demons. Stella's smoking was directly attached to her drinking, and drinking had caused her a lot of problems. Those problems all had consequences.

The thought of Christmas for Stella didn't even register. Her cell phone rang. "Hello."

"Stella?"

"Who's asking?"

"Stella, it's me, Molly."

"Oh."

"Do you want to pick up a little work?"

Stella contracted for Molly fairly often. Molly paid decent, and she paid in cash. She even gave her some up-front money now and then.

"Sure, Molly. What do you need?"

"This one is going to pay a little more, Stella, but it is crucial that no one finds out about it."

"Who would I tell?" Stella didn't really have friends that would care about any of the cases Molly had. Molly's clients and Stella's friends didn't exactly travel in the same circles.

"Okay, meet me in the office at 5 o'clock. You need to be dressed nice. You are going to a book signing."

● ● ●

John started getting ready. He stood in the walk-in closet and stared at a row of tuxes. Hanging next to them were all of his suits. As he looked at them, he decided a pinstripe with a black shirt and black tie would look sharp. It had kind of a bad-boy look, but it still had a professional flavor to it.

Book signings were okay. They had to be done. He actually liked meeting his readers. The snow might put a damper on things; it might cause his fans to stay home. Hopefully, the number of Christmas shoppers would offset the bad weather.

Nights like this made him want to stay inside

by the fire. His fireplace was huge. He often fell asleep in front of it while the fire roared. Tonight was made for that.

As he finished getting ready, the limo from his publisher pulled up to take him to the signing. They had really been putting forth extra effort since he hadn't re-signed with them yet. John was bored and tired of everything. It wasn't the publisher's fault. He just felt restless; maybe he would just quit and not sign with anyone.

As the limo pulled around his circle drive, he looked out the window and thought about how much he loved this house. It had been custom-built after he lost his parents. It was a log home made with huge, round logs, and almost every room had a rock fireplace. The rustic décor gave it a masculine feel, while keeping the warmth of a winter lodge. He liked the fact that it looked like it was set back in time, yet had the most modern of conveniences. His favorite feature was the rock fireplace outside on the wrap-around porch. It was the biggest of the fireplaces and put out an enormous amount of heat. Since that part of the porch was covered, he could take his thoughts and coffee outside, even in the snow. He had done some of his best work in front of that fireplace.

He had a lot to think about. His cabin had one thing missing—someone to love him.

● ● ●

Noelle finished some of her shopping and headed home. Tonight she needed to get some decent sleep, because she would have to answer Roger's questions tomorrow and needed a clear head.

Once inside the penthouse, she took a hot bath. It felt wonderful! Her feet still hurt from wearing those shoes last night, and shopping had not helped. When she got out of the tub, she wrapped up in a thick white robe, threw her hair up in a towel, and sat down in her favorite chair with a deep mug of hot chocolate.

Before long Noelle had dozed off. As she dreamed, she was at a party. John Brittingham held her in his arms, and they were waltzing. Her feet barely skimmed the floor, and he hadn't taken his eyes off her. He couldn't. Those black eyes of his just locked into her green ones. One, two, three ... One, two, three ...

She woke up startled. Why couldn't she quit thinking of him? It wasn't as if she was working out a plan. Those eyes just kept teasing her. *This has to stop,* she told herself. He didn't even know she was alive.

She got up to dry her hair and clear her thoughts. Christmas was taking its toll on her. She looked out of her bedroom window and wondered what Molly had found out.

Time was not Noelle's friend.

● ● ●

Stella arrived at Molly's office about ten minutes after 5:00. As she strolled in, Molly seemed irritated.

"You're late."

"Traffic."

"Yeah, I'm sure. Sit down—we're in a hurry."

"You'll be going to a book signing tonight. Once you are there, you will try to meet the author. You goal is to get a date with him."

"Why?"

"When you arrange the date, my client will show up instead of you. It will give her the access she needs to make a business deal. Got it?"

"Seems simple enough."

"We'll see. There is a car and driver waiting for you downstairs. Here's a copy of the book. Read the jacket while you're on the way so you will have something to talk about."

Stella took the book and went downstairs to the car. As she flipped through the book, she recognized the author's picture. *John Brittingham?* Molly had to be kidding!

She stepped into the car and pulled out her mirror to check her lipstick. Stella looked great. Her sweater and skirt were a soft winter white. The matching fur collar around the sweater's neckline flawlessly complimented it. Her pearl earrings and her slinky pumps looked stunning. She had topped it all off with a significant diamond ring that she wore on her right hand. No one would ever suspect that she was broke.

She stepped out of the car in front of the bookstore where a line was starting to form. That would not do. She needed to be at the front of the line.

With the appearance of authority, she walked toward the author's signing table. The store had placed the table next to the travel section. Perfect! She strolled up, as closely as possible—next to where John Brittingham was seated. Casually, though intentionally, Stella bent down and picked up a book about Paris from a lower shelf. As she reached down, she oh-so-carefully stretched her long and shapely leg out for John to notice, and he did.

As he continued to sign and visit with fans, he kept cutting his eyes in her direction. She could sense his hot stare as she browsed, being ever so cautious not to return his attention. After about ten minutes or so, she thought it was time make her move. She waited until he was in a conversation, and then blended into the line of people. She could tell he was searching for her. Stella liked watching his eyes dart about frantically. It was almost comical to see him trying to be polite but curt with the readers. He had lost interest in what he was doing.

As the line moved forward, John spotted her.

His entire countenance changed. His body visibly relaxed.

"Would you mind signing my book? I really admire your work," Stella asked in her throatiest of voices. She thought he was going to physically stand up and send all the other readers home. He was an attentive audience.

"Not at all. May I ask to whom you would like this made out?"

"Stella."

"Do you have a last name, Stella?"

"Just Stella."

"You know, 'just Stella,' since you're such a big fan, I would like to do something special for you."

"Really?" Stella feigned surprise.

"I will be through in about 45 minutes. Would you consider having dinner with me?"

"Well, Mr. Brittingham, I hardly know you."

"Fair enough. We will be chaperoned by my limo driver. How does that sound?"

"I'll meet you. Let's say The Bistro at 10:00. Do you know where that is, Mr. Brittingham?"

"I do know, and 10:00 is fine, but call me John. After all, I don't know your last name."

"Ten o'clock it is. Good-bye, John."

"Good-bye, Stella."

This was a little more complicated than she had bargained for. It was too late to have the client show up. She would just have to meet with him herself this time. Surely Molly would understand.

She asked the driver to take her down the road to The Bistro, and then she sent him home. She didn't really want Molly to find out from the driver that she had a date with John Brittingham. Anyway, it wouldn't matter after tonight. Maybe she would have the opportunity to find out more about his schedule. She could just take a taxi home. At least she thought she could . . .

As Stella began her night, Noelle fell fast asleep.

● ● ●

Stella settled down at a table with John's book. *The King's Men and the Queen's Ladies* was a number one best seller. It said so right on the book jacket. She looked through the chapter titles and read the jacket information. She even decided she would skim through the pages.

Stella wasn't exactly what one would call "a reader." She had the viewpoint that if something was good, it would eventually come out as a movie.

What could this guy find to write about anyway? Sooner or later, he has to run out of stuff, she thought to herself.

She was flipping through the pages when John

walked up behind her. "Did you find something good to read?"

"Sure. I can't wait. Are you through signing books?"

"For tonight. Let's find out a little about you, Beautiful."

"How original! Did you just create that line, my new writer friend?"

"Not really, but did it work?"

"Not really, but you can keep trying. I wouldn't dream of stopping you. Seriously, why did you single me out for dinner?"

"You're beautiful, and you have great taste in books!"

"Touché. I bow to your finesse."

As the evening went on, the two grew closer. "Would you like to come to my house and have a cup of coffee?" asked John.

"That sounds lovely, but again, I don't know you very well."

"Again, my chauffeur can stay with us. Besides, you don't even have to come into the house. We'll sit outside by the fireplace."

"You have an outdoor fireplace?"

"Wanna' see it?"

Stella knew this was a mistake, but a night out sounded fun. She would worry about the consequences later, as usual.

● ● ●

The car pulled slowly down the long drive. The outside lights glistened off the freshly-fallen snow, causing a reflection in the horizon.

There it was, right in the front of the house—the largest fireplace she had ever seen. In fact, it was one of the biggest houses she had ever seen. For the first time in a long time, she was actually looking forward to something. This guy seemed different. His lifestyle was different anyway.

Most of the men she had dated were losers. They had no dreams, no goals. Not this guy. Somehow, he had made his dreams come true. Being around him made Stella feel like her dreams could come true too. Her only problem was that her dreams had long ago been forgotten. As they rode in silence, she thought back to when she was a little girl. What had she wanted to become when she grew up? Oh, yes, she remembered. Stella had wanted to be a nurse. In her heart of hearts, she liked the way it felt when she did something nice for someone else. She hadn't had that feeling for years.

"What are you thinking about?" asked John.

"Oh, nothing really."

"You seemed pretty lost in your thoughts. Are you sorry you came with me?"

"Of course not. I was just thinking how wonderful you are."

"I see. What if I told you that I don't believe you?"

"Mr. Brittingham, you would be calling me a liar, I do believe," she answered in her most exaggerated Southern drawl.

"Well, that wouldn't be very polite of me so I must choose to take you at your word and most graciously accept your flattery. Tell me something else about yourself. For instance, what do you do for a living?"

Stella felt a twinge of guilt as she answered. "I'm an investor."

"An investor? What do you invest in?"

"The future, Darling. I always invest in the future."

Silence fell over the car again as it rolled up slowly in front of the huge porch. As if appearing from nowhere, the chauffer quickly opened Stella's door, waiting for her to step out. He took her hand as she reached for the door to keep her balance. And just as quickly as he came, he was gone again. The long, shiny car left them standing in the drive, surrounded by the deafening hush of the lightly falling snow. Stella probably should have been nervous out in the woods with this almost stranger, but she wasn't.

She actually felt safer than she had in months, especially the last few months.

John held out his arm for her to hold as they ascended the gradually inclining rock steps toward the fireplace. It was roaring, and she felt the heat of the fire and of the moment spread over her.

The fireplace angled out, allowing them to sit in front of the fire while looking out over the snow-covered acreage. They rocked in the wooden glider, neither one talking. They didn't touch or look at each other; each absorbed in their own thoughts. Stella knew guys like this didn't fall for women like her. But tonight, just for tonight . . .

*The swift wind of compromise
is a lot more devastating
than the sudden jolt of misfortune.*

CHARLES R. SWINDOLL

4

Noelle called Molly Red on her way into work. Roger was going to want to know about the meeting she had with the Board.

"Molly Red. Please leave a message after the tone." All Noelle got was the machine.

Great, just great, she thought to herself.

● ● ●

"Stella, it's Molly. What happened last night?"

"Not much."

"What do you mean, 'not much'?"

"Just what I said. Not much. I went to the book signing and met him."

"The driver said he dropped you at a restaurant."

"So?" Stella answered.

"Why?"

"Why, what?"

"Why did the driver drop you? You were supposed to call me. How did you get home?" Molly was getting irritated and was tired of playing Stella's game. "If you expect to get paid, Stella, you better start talking to me."

"All right, calm down. It is no big deal. I went to the book signing, I met John Brittingham, and I left. It was too late to have you call the client. So what?"

"Did you leave by yourself?"

"I'm sure the driver has already told you that I did."

"Knock it off, Stella. Did you set up a meeting with John or not?"

"That was the agreement. I am suppose to meet him for coffee tonight at 7:00. He's going to be Christmas shopping at the mall. We are meeting at the coffee bar inside the mall. Will that work for you, Ms. Red?"

"It's about time. I'll call the client. Oh, and Stella, you will need to show up. I'll have the client, Noelle Reynolds, approach you in the coffee shop. She can be the friend you haven't seen in a while. Is everything clear?"

"Crystal." Stella hung up the phone without saying goodbye. There had been no point in telling

Molly about last night. Molly was wound a little tight for Stella's taste anyway. Think how mad she would be if she knew Stella was meeting John at 5:00 for dinner before they were to go shopping at the mall.

● ● ●

"Noelle Reynolds," she answered as she picked up her cell phone.

"Noelle? It's Molly Red. We have a plan in place. My co-worker is meeting Mr. Brittingham at the coffee bar inside the mall at 7:00. You are to approach the two of them and pretend that she is an old friend who you haven't seen in the last few years."

"Wow. That was fast, Molly. Thanks, I'll be there."

"The rest is up to you."

● ● ●

As Noelle walked into the office, her face was beaming. Jacqui couldn't help but notice the change in her countenance.

"My, my! Don't you seem to have the Christmas spirit?" Jacqui exclaimed as she smiled at Noelle.

"Almost, my dear friend. Things are looking up. Has Roger called me yet?"

"Yes. He wants to know about the Board meeting. He'll call back about 2:00 this afternoon."

"Jacqui, I have an author coming in to sign a contract at 2:00. Would you do me a huge favor? Tell Roger I'll try to call him tonight, but let him know the Board wants us to sign John Brittingham as soon as possible. They want a rush put on the deal. Let him know that I have been working on it, and I will be meeting with the notorious Mr. Brittingham at 7:00 this evening!"

"Oh, my gosh, Noelle! How? How did you get a meeting?"

"It's a long story, and I have a lot to do so I'll tell you more later. I need to make sure I'm ready. Would you get me the company car for tonight? Oh, and a driver too!"

"Done. He will pick you up at 6:30. How does that sound?"

"Actually, have him pick me up at 4:30. I have to finish my shopping tonight, and I might as well be dropped at the door. Will that work?"

"Your chariot will arrive at 4:30, your Majesty!" Jacqui laughed as she teased her boss. She liked Noelle so much that it was easy to be happy for her successes.

● ● ●

Noelle picked the appropriate outfit, not too dressy. After all, she was supposed to be a Christmas shopper. Not too casual—she needed to make a good impression.

The car and driver arrived at 4:30, just as promised. As Noelle stepped inside, her heart and hopes soared high.

● ● ●

Stella had told John she would meet him at the restaurant. She definitely couldn't let him see her "house." He thought she had money and that she was well traveled. Nothing could have been further from the truth, but the truth would have to stay hidden awhile longer.

She arrived at the restaurant a little early and asked to be seated. The waiter placed her in a secluded spot at her request.

John arrived a few moments later, guided by the waiter to her table. "Hello, Stella. You look beautiful."

"Mr. Brittingham, you look pretty dashing yourself."

"Are you ready to face the Christmas rush?"

"I've looked forward to it all day." Stella was telling the truth. She had thought about this moment all during the day. She wanted it to be real. She had been imagining an ending different from the one that would play out.

As they ate their meal and talked, she longed for everything to be real. Stella wanted to be the person he was interested in getting to know, at least as long as her dream lasted.

● ● ●

John was drawn to Stella. She was sexy and interesting. Weren't they all? Christmas still felt lonely, even with a beautiful face staring at him from across a candlelit table. Stella Stone would get him through the season, but she would not be around when the snow melted.

It wasn't anything Stella was doing wrong; she seemed to know and do all the right things. She just didn't fill his heart. The emptiness still gnawed at him.

The meal went by with relative uneventfulness, and they headed toward the car to start an evening of Christmas adventure. Suddenly, Stella sprang a new idea on him. "John, have you ever been to the Art Center Museum Shop?"

"No, I don't think so. What is it?"

"At the art museum, there is a gift shop that has some unusual gifts. Would you want to look there first?"

"I guess. That sounds kind of different. I don't have much to buy anyway."

UNHINGED

"If you don't like it, we'll go on to the mall. How does that sound?"

"I'll be honest, Stella. The mall almost never sounds good to me."

"Let's make an evening of it!"

As the car headed for the museum, the two snuggled down in the back seat.

● ● ●

Noelle was able to get much of her shopping completed while she waited on her mark to enter the coffee bar. At around 6:45, she headed toward the chosen rendezvous spot. A hot drink and comfortable seat actually felt good in the middle of the Christmas panic.

It was ten minutes after seven. Where could they be?

Seven thirty-five.

At eight, Noelle realized the moment was gone. They weren't coming.

She picked up the phone and called Molly. "Molly, this is Noelle. Where are they?"

"They should be there by now."

"They never showed. Molly, this is getting serious. Find out where they are and call me back."

"I'll check on them right now. Sit tight, and we'll get this resolved." As she hung up the phone, Molly Red knew something had gone wrong. Stella could usually be counted on because she was all about the dollar. Money usually kept Stella on whatever track held the money.

She immediately started trying to reach Stella, but to no avail. Stella wasn't answering. As she called Noelle to tell her the bad news, she knew things were probably worse than they appeared.

Stella would pay for this one.

● ● ●

When Jacqui saw Noelle's face the next morning, she knew things had not gone well.

"What happened?" asked Jacqui.

"He didn't show up."

"You're kidding!"

"In all fairness, I didn't have an actual meeting set up with him. I was going to trick him into a meeting. I guess the joke was on me. What am I going to tell Roger?"

"Well, Roger thinks you met John last night. He is flying to a conference in China today. He said he would touch base with you after the conference. That should give you another four days before he checks in again."

"Four days, four years. I'm sunk, Jacqui."

"Maybe not. You know, I really believe God can make a way when everything looks impossible, Noelle."

"You always say things like that, Jacqui. Do you honestly believe God even cares about things like this? I think He has bigger things to be concerned about . . . world peace, sick people, you know, things that change world events. My job isn't exactly world changing."

"That isn't the point, Noelle. The point is that God cares about you. He cares about your desires, your dreams, and He longs to have a personal relationship with you."

"I can't even get a meeting with John Brittingham. How would I get to know God personally?" Her face smirked just a little as she closed the conversation, and Jacqui knew she had said enough.

● ● ●

John dropped Stella at a hotel downtown. She told him that she was staying there while her home was being remodeled. He instantly offered to let her stay in his guesthouse for the remainder of her remodel.

It was a temptation Stella couldn't pass up. She said she would bring her things in the morning to settle in for a week or two . . . or three.

As John pulled away from the hotel, he knew he had made a mistake. It would be harder to get rid of her now.

● ● ●

Stella couldn't believe her good fortune. Molly would probably fire her, but she didn't care! If she played her cards right, she would never have to worry about money again. John Brittingham held the keys to her future in his hands. Nothing had ever gone right for Stella, and this was the break she had been waiting for. She wouldn't let it pass by so easily. She wanted to grab the brass ring, or gold ring perhaps, and she would hold on for dear life.

As she hailed a taxi to take her to her little dive of a house, she had big plans. Things would be different now. Time had swung the pendulum in her favor. She would have to be careful. A double life was like a double-edged sword. It could make a way for her, or it could slice her to ribbons.

● ● ●

John entered the empty house. Stella would move into his guesthouse tomorrow. He didn't even know her, not really. It didn't matter. He was just killing time. It made him hate himself on the inside. What kind of man had he become?

His parents had been married for years. They had a real marriage, the unconditional kind. They were faithful and honest. What kind of person would want to marry him now with his reputation? The kind of wife he wanted would never tolerate his sordid past.

He sat up alone that night and thought about

what his life should have been like. What was the point of this big home if he didn't have someone to share it with, someone who mattered to his stony heart?

There was no one who knew the real John Brittingham. No one knew of the longings deep in his soul. No one even tried to know.

Before he went to bed, he left a note for the maid to make sure the guesthouse had everything ready for company.

He intended to sleep in.

> *People don't have fortunes left them
> in that style nowadays;
> men have to work
> and women to marry for money.
> It's a dreadfully unjust world.*
>
> LOUISA MAY ALCOTT

5

Stella pulled her sports car under the covered area that extended out over the drive. As she knocked on the front door, she felt a sense of arrival. She was good when it came to men. Men liked her, and this one was no different. By the time she was finished with him, this would all be hers, with or without John Brittingham.

After a servant answered the door, Stella asked for John. The older woman answered quietly, "Master Brittingham is engaged in business at the moment. He has asked that I show you to the guesthouse. He will call for you as soon as he is available."

Her answer caught Stella a little off guard. On the other hand, successful people were busy people. John had important things to do. She understood his predicament. At least she thought she did.

• • •

Molly kept trying to call Stella. No answer.

As far as Molly was concerned, Stella was finished. Molly would have to come up with a different plan. She decided she would have to handle things herself.

Molly put on a tailored gray suit and started toward John Brittingham's house. She hoped she would be able to come up with an idea by the time she arrived.

She wasn't sure if there was security at his home; however, she anticipated needing a good story.

Her anticipation was unfounded.

• • •

Time was closing in on Noelle. She decided it was time to meet John Brittingham on her own terms. She was completely sick and tired of being at his beck and call. The problem was, he never called.

She put on her most professional suit, and she headed out to the address Molly had given her.

• • •

John finally came to the guesthouse. It was almost 3:00 in the afternoon, and Stella had settled in comfortably.

"Welcome, neighbor," said John.

"Hi, stranger. What are you doing in this neck of the woods?"

"I heard there was a beautiful maiden who was kept locked in a guesthouse by an old, mean author. I came to rescue her."

"Maybe the beautiful maiden will simply pull him into the house with her, and they will stay locked up for eternity."

"Maybe the ending hasn't been written yet. Hey, how about a late lunch? Are you hungry?"

"Sure. I had a drink out by the pool earlier, but it has worn off. Let me change, and I'll be ready."

"No problem. I'll go tell Maria that you will be having lunch with us. Meet me in the dining room."

As John left, Stella felt a hesitation in him.

● ● ●

As both Molly and Noelle set their courses for John Brittingham's house, Stella was making herself at home. She walked across the path to the veranda entry.

"Hello?" As she stepped inside, she was taken aback at the grandiose nature of John's home. The furniture was made of hand-hewn logs, just as you would find in the finest of mountain resorts.

"Hello?" Stella repeated.

"In here, Stella," John answered. Stella wondered into the spacious dining room. The table was long and made from a thick slice of stained oak. There were two places set at the table, and John was already seated. Papers were scattered out in front of him.

"Hi. Am I interrupting anything?" Stella asked.

"No, I was just looking over the contract my publisher is offering me."

"Really?" Stella tried to act surprised.

"I'm not sure yet what I want to do."

"Why not?"

"There are several reasons, I guess. Hey, let's quit talking business. How do you like the guesthouse?" John didn't see any reason to share anything further with Stella. She wouldn't be around to see the outcome anyway.

"I love my new home." Stella answered him with actual appreciation in her voice. She honestly did love the place. She loved everything about being at John's ranch. Stella looked over at John, smiled, and touched his hand.

John nodded, but he didn't smile or return her touch. The house already felt too cramped, and he felt smothered.

● ● ●

Molly pulled onto the road leading to John's driveway. She was about a quarter of a mile from his house, when another car started following her.

UNHINGED

Looking in the rearview mirror, she could see Noelle. Molly slowed down and signaled for Noelle to pull over.

"What are you doing out here?" Molly nervously asked.

"Well, Molly, you really haven't been able to help me. I decided to take matters into my own hands."

"I'm sure we'll get this handled today, Noelle."

"Molly, I'm sorry. I just can't let it go any further. You are too expensive, and you're not getting any results. I'm going to have to let you go."

"Noelle, I think you are making a real mistake. How will you do this on your own?"

"I don't know, but I have to try."

"I understand." Molly got in her car and headed back to the city.

Stella could not have been more fired.

● ● ●

After Molly left, Noelle continued toward the house. As she pulled into the drive, she noticed a gate not far from the entrance. She pulled the car up to the intercom and pressed the button.

"May I help you?"

"I'm here to see John Brittingham."

"May I announce your visit?"

Announce my visit? Good grief, this guy is spoiled,

73

Noelle thought to herself. "Yes, please announce my visit. My name is Noelle Reynolds."

"Personal or business?"

Noelle knew she was about to hit a wall. "Business."

"The name of your company, please?"

"The Queen's House Publishing."

Several moments passed. Eventually, the woman came back with the inevitable news. "I'm sorry. Mr. Brittingham is unavailable."

"Will you please let him know that I came to see him?"

"Of course."

"May I leave a number?"

"If you wish."

Noelle gave her the number; however, she knew she would never receive a call. She had left her number many times before. "Thank you."

Noelle drove off feeling ridiculous. John Brittingham would never get that message, and she was probably going to lose her job.

● ● ●

When Noelle returned to the office, Jacqui appeared to be crying. She looked at Noelle and started sobbing even harder.

"Jacqui, you're scaring me. What's wrong?"

"Noelle, it's bad."

"Jacqui, tell me!"

"It's Roger. There was a car accident in China. He was in a taxi, and the driver lost control of the car. Noelle, Roger is dead."

Noelle sat down in disbelief. "No. Jacqui, are you sure? You know, sometimes people make mistakes. No one in China really knows him or the people with him. What if the authorities got their identities mixed up? I've seen shows where that happened. I mean, we really don't know for sure."

"Everyone in the taxi was killed. Roger had his wallet with his driver's license and his credit cards in his pocket. His passport was in the jacket he was wearing."

"Oh God, help me," Noelle cried out in desperation. Roger was a good manager and a good friend. They had worked many long hours together and had seen enormous success and worked through a few small failures. Life would be different without Roger.

"I guess they have told his wife?"

"The police told her this morning. She asked them to contact us."

"I should notify the rest of the Board." Since Noelle was temporarily in charge, everything would fall on her shoulders until the Board found a replacement. Pursuing John would have to take a back seat until the Board could get things under control.

Noelle gave Jacqui a hug, went into her office, and wept.

• • •

John walked into the great room where Maria was cleaning.

"Who was at the gate, Maria?"

"Just some lady trying to sell you something. I sent her away."

"Thanks, Maria. You're too good to me."

"You're right!" She looked at him and smiled, with a quick wink.

John told Stella he had some work to do, and he sent her back to the guesthouse. Although she had her own car, he told her she could borrow one of his cars if she wanted to go into the city. He hoped the temptation would be too great for her to refuse. At least if she went into the city, she would be out of his hair and out of his space.

John went into his office to work on his book. As he looked at the computer, he selected the "security" feature. John was able to view the film footage of various cameras around his property. It was just a little safety feature he had installed for when he happened to be there by himself.

As he looked at the gate-cam, he thought he might as well look at the tape of the visitor who came by earlier. When he rewound the tape, he stopped and looked again. The woman in the car was the woman from the Christmas party. He listened to the audio of the tape. She was from a publishing house? Of course, that's why she was at the party. It all made sense to him. He jotted down the number she had left on the tape.

Why had he ever let Stella move in?

● ● ●

After Roger's funeral had passed, the Board held an emergency meeting, and they asked to meet with Noelle shortly afterward. This time she was on time.

"Ms. Reynolds, we are sorry for the loss of your co-worker and friend. Roger was an excellent businessman. He will be missed, and he will be hard to replace. That being said, we have to keep The Queen's House Publishing moving forward. Therefore, we need to move quickly to maintain a composed transfer of assignment."

"I understand."

"In all actuality, you may not be the most qualified candidate for the position that Roger held, yet you are the best choice for the position. There will be less turmoil and disruption with you filling his shoes. You are current on his files, and you have the best chance of moving us forward. It is no secret that we want to increase profits, and you are quite capable of making that happen. Therefore, if you will accept, we would like to offer you the position as senior editor at The Queen's House Publishing."

Noelle couldn't believe it. Last week she was sure she was going to lose her job. Today she was being offered a promotion.

"I—I don't know what to say. Of course, I'll accept. Thank you."

Her joy was bittersweet as she thought about Roger. In addition, there was John Brittingham. Would they be this pleased with her if she couldn't get him to sign? She quickly put thoughts of him out of her mind. She wanted to enjoy the rest of the day. In spite of the sadness about Roger, she felt relieved to still have a job.

She had to make the most of this opportunity. The Board wasn't really sold on her, but she would change that. Noelle would make sure it was the best decision they ever made.

● ● ●

Stella pulled the car under the carport by the guesthouse. She had bought a small gift for John. She had already stayed at his house for a week, and time was passing quickly. He wasn't being nearly as friendly as she had anticipated. She thought by now that she would be in the main house. Maybe her little "gift" today would help.

Stella didn't stop by the guesthouse. She went straight in, through the veranda, into the great room, and then she went to find Maria. For some reason, she didn't feel comfortable approaching John without Maria's permission. Stella finally found her in the kitchen preparing dinner.

"Maria, do you know where John is?"

"Mr. Brittingham is probably in his office. He works in there most of the day. Sometimes he works on the porch by the fireplace."

Stella headed toward his office. With a quick peek inside, she saw he wasn't there. She walked through the great room to get to the porch. On her way through, she grabbed a couple of drinking glasses and a corkscrew.

She looked out on the porch and saw John with his laptop, next to a roaring fire. It was chilly outside, but when she stepped into the fire's heat, she immediately started to warm up. John looked good this evening. He looked at home and relaxed. Tonight might be the right time to make her move.

"Hey."

"Hey, Stella. Have a seat."

"I don't want to bother you."

"I need a break. What have you been up to today?"

"Well, I did a tiny bit of shopping."

"Sounds fun. Did you finish your Christmas shopping?"

"Yes, and I want to give you your present now."

"Stella, really, you shouldn't have."

"No, I insist. You've been so good to me. It is the least I can do." She sat a tall, narrow gift bag in front of him and put the two glasses on the table. "Go ahead; open it."

John looked at the bag suspiciously. As he reached into the bag, he felt the cool glass bottle under the tissue paper.

"It's a bottle of 1961 Yalumba Galway Claret," Stella said.

"Wow. That must have been expensive, Stella. Are you sure you want to give me this?"

"I'm positive. Let's open it and celebrate our new friendship."

"Stella, not to hurt your feelings and not that I don't appreciate it, but I don't drink anymore. Since my parents were killed by that drunk driver, I just haven't had a drink. I'm so sorry. I don't want to make you feel bad or embarrassed."

"Oh, I understand. No problem." She sat silently for a minute, looking at the bottle.

"Do you want to take the bottle back? I hate that it was so expensive." Stella knew that wasn't an option, because she had traded for it at the liquor store—her phone number for the bottle.

"No, that's silly. Do you mind if I have a drink?"

"Help yourself."

Stella poured herself a glass. It warmed her on the inside just as the fire warmed her on the outside. She had needed a drink for quite some time, and it felt good. She drank the first one down quickly, and then she poured another one. Only a few moments had passed before that glass was empty too.

"How about moving over to the glider?" Stella coaxed him. Stella was a looker, but he had been acting put off because she had been lingering around just a little too much. Under the overhang, with the fire reflecting across her face, she looked stunning.

John stood up, and in silence, he moved to sit down beside her. She snuggled in close and placed her hand on his chest. She finished her third glass of wine and started kissing his neck. It had been awhile since a woman had touched him, and he had missed it. He pulled her in and held her tightly against him.

"Stella, I need you to tell me why you are here," he whispered.

"I want to be with you. I want to touch you and hold you."

"Why me, Stella?" His eyes pierced hers. He had never been this serious in his life.

The wine had started taking over. Stella started giggling. "Come on, Baby. Can't we just have fun?"

John longed for someone to have fun with, but Stella's drinking was only fun for Stella. A month ago he wouldn't have cared whether his date had too much to drink, but tonight he felt differently. Even with her trying to seduce him, he felt lonely.

"Stella, I think it's time for me to get back to work."

Stella stood up, took what was left of the bottle, and went back to the guesthouse. He would pay for this. She was good at getting her way, and he deserved whatever happened to him. After all, he invited her to live at his home.

Inside the guesthouse, she picked up the phone and called a friend. "Billy, I need a favor."

"I ain't got no money, Stell."

"I don't want money. I need to borrow that camera you have, the one that records people without them knowing about it."

"Okay, you need me to bring it to you?"

"No, I'll come and get it tomorrow."

As Stella hung up the phone, she couldn't quit thinking about how John had made her feel foolish and small. She had been nothing but nice to him. He would regret the day he ever met Stella Stone.

Never wound a snake; kill it.

HARRIET TUBMAN

6

Jacqui arrived at the office early on December 20. When she checked the voice mail, she was shocked at the message that had been left on the machine.

"This is John Brittingham. I am trying to reach Noelle Reynolds' extension." He proceeded to leave several different numbers where he could be reached.

Jacqui hung up the phone. God had been good to them today, and the day was just getting started. She hurriedly called Noelle's cell phone.

"Hello."

"Noelle, I have a huge surprise for you—huge!"

"What?"

"Can't tell you yet. How close are you to the office?"

"About 15 minutes out. Tell me, Jacqui."

"Nope. See you in a few minutes." Jacqui hung up the phone before Noelle could argue and beg anymore.

What could she be talking about? wondered Noelle.

● ● ●

Noelle couldn't get to the office fast enough. The taxi dropped her right at the front door, and she raced to the elevator. Every person that got on and off seemed to be taking his time.

When Noelle got to the office, Jacqui was smiling from ear to ear. "What's going on?"

"We had an important message on the voice mail this morning."

Noelle physically dropped her shoulders and looked down. Everything about her body looked disappointed. "A voice mail? All this about a voice mail? Jacqui, you had me all excited. I thought it was something big."

" 'Beauty is in the eye of the beholder,' I guess."

"What do you mean?"

"Well, for instance, I thought John Brittingham was pretty big."

"John Brittingham? Jacqui, if you're joking, this isn't the time."

"Oh, Noelle, he called. He asked for you personally. He wanted to leave a message on your extension. He left several numbers for you to call him—his personal numbers."

"Oh, Jacqui. How could I be this lucky? I never thought this would happen in a million years."

Jacqui stopped for a moment and looked at Noelle. "Lucky? Noelle, the chances of this being luck are one in a million. Don't you see?"

"See . . . what?"

"Noelle, I have been praying for this every day since the Board told you that they wanted you to sign him. This isn't luck. I told you that God would make a way."

"Jacqui, I truly appreciate you thinking so much of me that you would take time to pray for me, but I can't believe God would even care about this."

"Noelle, in the Bible, Jesus looks over a crowd of people. In Matthew 9:36, God's Word says, 'When he saw the crowds, he had compassion on them, because they were harassed and helpless, like sheep without a shepherd.' Do you know what the word compassion means?"

"I guess. It means to feel sorry for someone or to feel sorry about his situation."

"Kind of. It means so much more, especially in this case. When Jesus had compassion for them, He felt what they felt. He felt their pain and suffering and confusion. He felt it so strongly that it almost made him physically ill to hurt for them so badly."

"I didn't know that."

"Noelle, whenever we have talked about God, you seem to think He would never care about your problems. Does the Jesus I just described sound like someone that wouldn't care about you, about your heart, about your needs?"

"I guess not."

"He loves you, Noelle, and He is waiting for you to love him back."

"I'm not sure I really understand, but I'll think about it."

She went into her office and dialed John's number.

● ● ●

"John Brittingham."

"Mr. Brittingham, this is Noelle Reynolds. I am returning your call."

"Hello, Ms. Reynolds. Listen, I want to apologize for missing you at my home yesterday afternoon. I normally ask not to be disturbed while I write."

"Oh, I'm so sorry."

"No, no. I just meant that I had no idea you were waiting to see me."

"No problem."

"Would it be possible for you to come back out and try it again this afternoon?"

"That sounds wonderful. What time?"

"Would you like to come for lunch?"

"I'll be there around 12:00."

"Ms. Reynolds, you never told me why you were here."

"Mr. Brittingham, you never asked." Noelle smiled as she hung up the phone. He was definitely charming. She would have to be careful with this one.

● ● ●

Stella met Billy in the city, picked up the camera, and headed back to John's house. She hadn't seen him since he embarrassed her the day before. He would have to come to her. She wasn't going to go to him.

Since John always wrote when he came in from running, she knew he wouldn't be in the great room. She snuck in, trying not to let Maria see her. The camera looked like a book. She could easily set it on the bookshelf, and it would blend with the other books. She tried to face it toward the center of the room.

When she had finished, she crept back over to the guesthouse. Hopefully, John would start feeling guilty about what had happened and would come and visit her. If not, she would have to figure out a way to get to him.

John Brittingham was king of his world, but she was ready and waiting to watch his kingdom crumble.

● ● ●

"Maria, I'm having a special guest for lunch today," John told her, as she walked past his office door.

"What shall I prepare?"

"How about something warm? Do you have any stew made up?"

"It will be ready at noon."

"Thanks, Maria."

John went back to working on his book. His time wasn't very productive. He kept watching the clock. At 11:00, he would get cleaned up and change into something presentable, something that she might like.

He knew why she wanted to see him, but he didn't care. All he cared about was the opportunity to meet her, to look into her eyes.

Time continued to drag by, and he didn't really get any writing done at all. It didn't matter today. Something about seeing her made his whole day better.

He almost had the Christmas spirit.

● ● ●

This time, when Noelle pulled into John Brittingham's drive, she got right inside. The gates swung open wide for her.

She arrived in front of the big log home. She hadn't seen anything like it except in magazines. She stepped onto the porch and knocked on the heavy wooden door. Maria answered it almost as she knocked.

"Good afternoon," Maria said.

"Good afternoon. I'm here to see Mr. Brittingham."

"Please come in. I will let him know you are here."

Noelle walked in and stood sheepishly in the foyer. How could it be so easy just to come inside his home today, when she couldn't get past the gate yesterday? She thought about what Jacqui said about God making a way.

"Good afternoon, Ms. Reynolds." John Brittingham came around the corner with the boyish smile. He was even better looking up close. Her heart was about to beat out of her chest.

"Hello, Mr. Brittingham."

"It's good to have you here on the B & B Ranch."

"The B & B Ranch?"

"Crazy, huh? Since I write books, I enjoy being able to work out here, but I don't have time to keep things running like a real ranch."

"What does B & B stand for?"

"Brittingham & Brittingham."

"Clever. Has this place been passed down through your family?"

"No, but I hope it will be someday."

"I didn't know you had any children."

"I don't, but I hope to eventually." He really didn't know why he was sharing so much with her so quickly. As he looked into her eyes, he just wanted to be open with her. He wanted her to know him. He hadn't cared what anyone thought about him for so long that he had almost forgotten how to be honest, even with himself.

"We'll be having lunch out on the porch, if you don't mind." She thought about how chilly it was outside. He could tell she was slightly hesitant.

"Don't worry. The fire will keep us warm." As they went outside, the air did indeed have a nip. However, as they sat down at the table, the roaring fireplace put out plenty of heat. It was easy to relax and her nerves calmed down.

The table was set beautifully. The dinnerware was decorated with different ranch brands, completing the motif. Even the napkins were red-checkered with small, rope lasso napkin rings.

He held out a chair for her. "The table is lovely," said Noelle.

"Thanks. Maria is very kind to help me. I couldn't make it without her."

They sat for several seconds not speaking. He couldn't take his eyes off her eyes. What he had seen across the room a few weeks ago was even more beautiful in the sunlight.

"Okay, I guess I should ask. Why did you come here yesterday?"

"I was hoping to talk to you about signing with The Queen's House Publishing."

"Hmm ... I don't know what I want to do."

"I'm sure your publisher is trying to get you to sign a new contract."

"Well, yes, but I haven't decided to sign yet."

"May I ask why not?"

"I wish I knew the answer to that question. I don't even know if it has anything to do with them. I've just had a lot to think about lately."

"I guess you've been working hard on your new book."

"I have been working hard, but there is more to it than that. I think I might be getting sentimental. I don't know. Maybe it's just the holiday season."

"What are doing for Christmas?" Noelle decided it might be beneficial to lighten the moment. Things had taken a serious turn, and she wasn't sure if he was feeling good about their meeting or not.

"I will probably be relaxing here at the ranch. What about you?"

"I have an apartment in the city. So much has happened in our office over the last couple of weeks that I had to cancel my trip home."

As the lunch progressed, the couple talked as if they had known each other forever. Maria came out and checked on them once, but they had privacy during most of the meal. When they had finished eating, Maria brought out two hot cups of coffee.

"Would you like to move over, closer to the fire?"

"Sure." As Noelle took a seat next to him, it felt natural. They talked like old friends. As they wound down the afternoon, John desperately wanted to see her again.

"Noelle, I know we haven't really talked business, and I know that is why you came here. I didn't intend to push that to the side. I would be happy to come to you and talk business, if you still want to. I was just enjoying the company."

"Of course, I would love to. I've had a great time too. Would you have time to come to my office tomorrow?"

"Name the time."

"How about 3:00?"

"We can get a bite to eat afterward if you would like."

Did he just ask me out? Noelle thought to herself. She wanted to stand up and cheer, but she very intentionally collected her emotions and said, "Yes, I'd like that."

Suddenly, Stella appeared on the porch, stumbling up a step as she approached them. Stella had obviously been drinking. The ashes from her cigarette fell onto the table.

"Hello, everyone. Did I miss the party?"

"Hello, Stella." John was not at all happy, but it was too late.

"What's your name, Missy?" Stella looked at Noelle. "You're a pretty thing."

"Noelle, this is Stella. Stella, this is Noelle. Is that better, Stella?"

"Pleased to make your acquaintance, Ms. Noelle."

"Thank you." Noelle looked slightly put off. John didn't like the look on Noelle's face. It made him uneasy. He wanted everything to be perfect.

"Stella, why don't we talk later? Noelle and

I have some business to take care of before she leaves."

"Business? Oh, I see. Business, something I wouldn't know anything about. Is that what you are trying to say?"

"Stella, I'm not saying anything. Please just wait for me inside."

"I'll wait for you, Darling. I always wait for you, don't I? I'm sorry if I've been rude. I'll make it up to you. You come and see me, Baby, when you're done."

"Stella! That's enough. Get in the house. Noelle, I am so sorry. She is drunk."

"I need to be going, John. I'll see you at the office tomorrow, and it's easy to see you have a lot going on right now. Maybe we should hold off on dinner. You seem to have your hands full."

John apologized again and walked Noelle to the car. He assured her that he would be in her office at 3 P.M. sharp. She wondered if he would show, but she had plenty to wonder about today.

● ● ●

John stormed back into the house and let Maria know that she could have the rest of the day off. Then he went to the great room to look for Stella.

"What got into you? What were you thinking?" He turned his back on her in total disgust.

She stood behind him, with a slack stance. Yet

he was still able to smell her foul breath, a mixture of cigarettes and bourbon. "Oh, lighten up, John. When I met you, I thought you were going to be a lot of fun. Well, guess what—you're not! You are boring! Boring John Brittingham. That should be your name. All you do is work. When you aren't working, you're thinking about working. It's stinkin' Christmastime, John. Christmas! Remember that holiday? You don't even have a stupid tree!"

In a flat-toned voice, John replied, "Get out, Stella. Just get out."

Then he turned to look at her. Somehow, in the midst of her yelling, she had started to unbutton her blouse. He quickly turned back around, facing away from her. She walked up and put her arm around his stomach, placing her head on his back.

He stood there for a moment with his head down. This was all his fault. He had started this whole thing by letting her move in. Some of his anger left when he thought about how he had not been the host she had expected.

He placed his hand over hers and held it for a moment. Then he turned around and faced her. He put his hands on her hips, and then slowly he tilted her face toward his and kissed her on the cheek, just beside her nose. He looked her in the eye and said, "Stella, it's time for you to go. I know this hasn't been what you intended, and I apologize for that. I should have never brought you here."

"Come on, John. You don't mean that. I'm sorry. Let's just start over."

"Stella, we never had anything to start with."

She slowly stepped back from him. "You can't blame a girl for trying. Before I leave, tell me who that woman was." John kind of smiled and shook his head.

"She's from The Queen's House Publishing. She was here trying to get me to sign a publishing contract." Stella wanted to laugh aloud. All this for nothing.

"You looked like it was more than business." John didn't answer her. "Let me get my book that I laid on the bookcase, and then I'll get the rest of my things gathered." She stepped around him and took the book off the shelf behind him.

"Stella, I really am sorry."

"Me too."

All Stella could think of was how sorry he would be.

*We know too much,
and are convinced of too little.
Our literature is a substitute for religion,
and so is our religion.*

T.S. ELIOT

7

Noelle and Jacqui planned to have lunch together. They wanted to get all their ducks in a row before John Brittingham came to the office, if he came. Since this was business, they went to a quiet place to plan wisely.

"What was he really like, Noelle?"

"That's hard to say Jacqui. I thought I was really connecting with him, but things just went south."

"What do you mean?"

"I told him who I worked for, and he seemed okay with it. He even asked me out!"

"You are kidding me! Are you going?"

"I was going to, but then this woman walked up."

"From where?"

"From his house. She apparently lives with him!"

"He is living with a woman, and he asked you out?"

"I guess we really shouldn't be surprised. We know what kind of life he leads."

"It's just such a waste. He is gorgeous!"

"I wanted to tell him that he made me sick, but I couldn't risk blowing the deal. He seemed pretty willing to sign."

"Did he like the terms in the contract?" asked Jacqui.

"That was the weirdest thing of all. He never looked at the contract. He never even asked about it."

"I have always heard truly creative people are eccentric. Maybe he is superstitious or something."

"Who knows?"

"Hey, Noelle, did you think about what we talked about a few days ago?"

"What did we talk about?"

"About God caring about you and making a way for you."

"Jacqui, that stuff is fine for you, but I don't know how I really feel about it."

"Does it make you feel awkward when we talk about God?"

"Not really, I just don't understand why it is so important to you, I guess."

"So what would have happened if you had been in that taxi with Roger?"

"Jacqui! That's awful! Don't talk like that."

"Noelle, I'm serious. You said you don't understand why it's so important to me so I'm telling you. Be honest. What would have happened if you had died that day?"

"I think St. Peter would let me in, if that's what you're asking."

"Something like that. Let me ask it a different way. What if you had been in that taxi? Instead of waking up in a hospital, you wake up in front of God Himself. As you stand there, God asks you, 'Why should I let you into my Heaven?' What would you say, Noelle?"

"Well, I've never done anything bad, not *really* bad anyway. I've always just done my best, and I've tried to be good to other people. If I know someone needs something, like food or money, I give it to them if I have it."

"Noelle, those are all really good things. Nothing would be wrong with living that kind of life. I can see why you would think that would be a good answer. I thought so too, at one time, but have you ever wondered about what God says He wants from you?"

"No, not really. I just thought He wanted me to be good."

"Well, He does, but He knows that no one can be good all the time. When God speaks of 'not being good,' He calls it sin. Not only is doing something bad a sin, but not doing something good that you know you should do—that's a sin too."

"Even if it is just a little sin?"

"Think of it this way, Noelle. When you park the company car in front of the building for too long without moving it, you get a parking ticket. If you get at least one ticket a month, in a year's time you would get 12 tickets. If you get 12 tickets a year for 25 years, you would have received 300 tickets at the end of that time. At that point, the judge has asked to see you. Do you think he will say, 'Three hundred tickets aren't *really* bad. Why don't you forget it, and I'll only convict murderers.' Do you think a *fair* judge, who has vowed an oath to enforce the law, would let that happen?"

"Probably not. I hadn't really thought about it like that."

"Now think about any small sins you may commit during the day. Do you ever have a bad thought? Do you ever watch something on TV that wouldn't please God? Do you ever say even one bad word? Have you ever avoided someone in need simply because you didn't have the time to deal with him?"

"I probably do at least three of those things a day."

"So three sins a day times 365 days in a year—that is 1095 sins in a year. Over a 70-year time span, you will have committed 76,650 sins."

"I never thought I was so bad."

"Do you want to face God with those charges being held against you?"

"Of course not, but I don't know if I can be any better. When I try hard to do the right thing, I can get better, but before long, I'm back to my old ways. Sometimes I'm even worse than I was before."

"God knows that Noelle. He knows we are all that way. That is why He made sure that our fine, our debt if you will, has already been paid. However, it is very personal. It is a gift He gives each of us."

"What do we have to do to get the gift?"

"That is what is so wonderful. All you have to do it accept the gift."

"How do I accept the gift?"

"That's the good part. See, sin has a punishment, and it separates us from God. We are sinful people, but He is a holy God. That puts a huge distance between God and us, like a giant chasm. God is on one side of the chasm, and we are on the other side of the chasm. Our sin is the chasm. We need a way to cross the chasm and get to God. Because of his love for us, He wants to be with us. He doesn't want sin to separate us from Him. Therefore, God sent Jesus to be the bridge from God to us. He is the way that we cross that great chasm. He was able to pay our debt by taking our punishment on the cross because He was without sin.

"Do you know what the word 'Lord' means, Noelle?"

"Not really. I thought it meant God."

"It actually means to let Him control your life, to live your life for him. Whatever is on the throne in your heart must be replaced with Jesus. For example, you said you thought your good behavior and good deeds would let you spend eternity with God. Your faith is in yourself. You must place that faith in what Christ did on the cross."

"I do believe in God."

"Noelle, do you know that the Bible says even demons believe in God? Do you think demons will be in Heaven?"

"I wouldn't think so. I'm not sure I understand the differences about believing."

"Okay, do you know Abe Lincoln?"

"Everyone knows Abraham Lincoln."

"Everyone may know who he was, but none of us actually *know* him. We only know *of* him. See the difference?"

"I think I do. I know about Abraham Lincoln,

but I don't have a personal relationship with Abraham Lincoln."

"I think you are getting it! Noelle, after Jesus died on the cross for you, for me, He rose to live again. He is alive now, and He sits at God's right hand. He is ready and willing to have that personal relationship with you."

"I haven't had a good relationship in a long time. It would be nice to have one with Someone who truly cares for me. If I ever want to tell Him that I want one too, what would I need to do?"

"You have to decide to give up your own way and choose his way. You have to take your faith and place it in Him alone. Prayer is like talking to Him. Talk to Him and tell Him you don't know how to pray. Ask Jesus to come into your heart. Tell Him the throne will be His from now on. Thank Him for dying in your place on the cross. Tell Him you will follow Him all the days of your life, no turning back."

"That is a lot to think about, Jacqui."

"It is the most important thing in the world, Noelle. Hey, I'm starved, what are we having?"

Noelle took everything Jacqui said and tucked it away into her heart.

● ● ●

Three o'clock seemed to roll around quickly, and just as he promised, John Brittingham was on time. Somehow, word of his arrival had leaked out, and paparazzi followed closely on his heels. He really didn't know what he was going to do, and he wished they wouldn't take pictures and spread rumors. He hadn't decided to leave his current publisher, and they were only making things more difficult.

"Mr. Brittingham, are you here to sign with The Queen's House Publishing?"

"I'm here to see a friend."

"Are you shopping for a new publisher?"

"I'm just here to see a friend. I've got to go. Thanks for asking." John tried to be polite. He knew that if he acted irritated that it would only feed the beast.

He looked great when he walked into The Queen's House Publishing, and he came bearing gifts. "I'm John Brittingham, and I'm here to see Noelle Reynolds."

He looked at Jacqui and flashed his charming smile. Jacqui was glad for Noelle's sake that he had showed up, but she wasn't crazy about John Brittingham. His reputation concerned her, and she knew that he had asked Noelle to dinner. Jacqui didn't trust him, but she was obligated to be polite to him.

"It's nice to meet to meet you, Mr. Brittingham."

"Please call me John."

"I'll let Ms. Reynolds know you are here."

UNHINGED

Within a few moments, Noelle buzzed for Jacqui and asked her to bring John back to her office. As he walked in, he smiled and extended his hand to Noelle. They lingered just a little longer than they normally would have, looking into each other's eyes.

"I hope you came to sign a contract, John."

"I came to see what you had to offer, Noelle. I brought you some autographed copies of some of my books, and these flowers are for you too."

Noelle was polite, but downplayed the gifts, not wanting to appear too emotional. John was charming, and she had to be careful. She didn't want to be lax, by turning over control of the meeting. "Thank you very much. Now let's get down to it. What will it take for you to switch publishers?"

"You make it sound pretty cut and dried. It's not that simple."

"Isn't it?"

"No, I've had several thoughts of not signing with anyone." They sat down on the sofa, which was under the window. John looked serious as he gazed outside.

"Why wouldn't you want to sign with someone?"

"Noelle, I'm kind of burned out. I couldn't even come here today without the press following me. Sometimes I feel like a prisoner in my own home."

"You seemed to have plenty of company." The

minute she said it, she wished she could take it back. It was none of her business.

"Noelle, I'm so sorry about yesterday. Stella was staying in my guesthouse. She does not live in the main house with me. She should have never been on my ranch at all. It was a mistake."

"What you do in your personal life isn't any of my business, John. I shouldn't have said anything. I was out of line. Please accept my apology. I just want to make sure you are able to write books."

"I'm glad you brought it up. I wanted to talk to you about it ever since it happened. I couldn't sleep last night thinking about it. I want you to believe me, Noelle. I don't know why it is so important to me, but I really want you to believe me."

Noelle studied his face, his eyes. He almost looked as if he were being truthful. He spoke so passionately that it was hard not to believe him. Of course, he made an extravagant living by creating words that seemed real. He was good at what he did.

"Let's look over the contract that Legal drew up. I'll assume there will be a few adjustments, which you will need to initial. When we have finished, I'll have Legal make the modifications, and a new contract will be brought to your home for you to sign."

"Only if you will bring it yourself."

"John, I really don't want to mix a personal situation with our business relationship."

"Only if you bring it yourself." John stuck firmly to his guns.

"Don't you think your house is a little crowded?"

"Noelle, I asked Stella to leave. She was drunk last night. I told you it was a mistake. She has moved out."

Noelle's heart skipped as he said it. *Oh, please let him be telling the truth,* she said to herself. On the outside, she kept up her all-business demeanor, and he just kept watching her, as if he could see her soul.

The price of anything is the amount of life you exchange for it.

HENRY DAVID THOREAU

8

When they had gone over all the contract ins and outs, there were only a few changes to be made. Actually, John hadn't been difficult at all, despite his reputation.

"Have you thought about going to grab a bite with me?"

"John, I told you that I don't like mixing business with pleasure. I don't think it is a good idea."

"Are you sure this doesn't have anything to do with Stella?"

"It might. I'm not sure."

"Noelle, I never even kissed Stella. We *never* had a physical relationship."

"I know about your reputation. That seems unlikely."

"I know what kind of reputation I have. It's

my own fault, but I hate it anyway. I am trying to change."

"I see. You are trying to change so you asked Stella to move in with you."

"Let me explain. I was at a book signing a few weeks ago. Stella appeared out of nowhere. Christmastime is usually a bummer for me because I don't really have any family. Sometimes I even dread this time of year. When I saw Stella at the book signing, I thought she might help get me through the holidays. I met her that night and asked her to go to dinner. It was late, and I'll admit, I thought she was beautiful. I asked her to come home with me, but we didn't sleep together. We just sat out by the fireplace and talked.

"After the evening came to a close, I took her to a hotel where she was staying. Her house was being remodeled so I offered to let her stay in my guesthouse. By the time the words were out of my mouth, I regretted it. Regardless, she moved in the next morning. I don't have any idea what got into me. I'll admit that I have been with some women, but I haven't been in the habit of asking them to move in. It was a mistake, Noelle."

"So why did you decide to ask her to leave?"

"I always thought sharing my home with someone would fill the void in my life. When she got there, I was lonelier than before she moved in."

"You can have anything you want, John. You can have anyone you want."

"That's just it, Noelle. I don't know what I want. No matter how much success I achieve, no matter how many women I sleep with, no matter what, I am never truly happy. Stella made me realize that a warm, beautiful body would not help me feel whole. Even with her willing offer of herself to me, I had a void in my heart."

"Why didn't you sleep with her if you slept with the others?"

"I guess I finally got sick of it all. I would still be alone the next day or whenever I got tired of her or she got tired of me. I know what you must think of me, but I knew there was something different about you that night at The Westminster. I never stopped thinking of you. I just had to meet you. Give me one more chance, please."

Noelle had so much to think about. John Brittingham would be easy to fall for.

"I'll go to dinner tonight, but I want our business relationship to stay separate. I will look out for the best interest of The Queen's House Publishing. Do you understand?"

"Completely. I have a beautiful place where we can go tonight. I think you'll like it, unless you have somewhere in particular you would like to go."

"As a matter of fact, I do. Are you ready for anything?"

"Sure!"

"Do you have a car downstairs?"

"Yes, but I'm sure reporters are hanging all over it."

Noelle pressed the intercom and asked Jacqui to have the company car pulled around. "We can leave from the private parking garage," Noelle told John.

Since taking over Roger's position, she had changed offices. Her new office provided easy access to the company garage and the company car. They rode in silence in the elevator, each wondering what the other was thinking.

Once inside the car, Noelle gave an address to the driver that John didn't recognize. She definitely had peaked his curiosity.

"Where are you taking me, Ms. Reynolds? I barely know you."

"Are you worried I am going to sully your reputation, Mr. Brittingham?"

"I'm a nice boy, and I don't want people to talk."

"I think it is time for you to broaden your horizons."

"That is kind of scary."

"We'll see what you are really made of."

The suspense was actually demanding his interest. He liked exciting women, and Noelle had a mind of her own.

The car drove into a secluded neighborhood. All he could see were regular houses. He couldn't imagine finding anything to do in a place like this. Gradually, the car came to a stop in front of a white bungalow.

"Where are we?"

"My aunt's."

"No offense, but this wasn't exactly what I had in mind."

"Be patient. You'll like it."

They got out of the car and walked up the drive to the side entrance. An older woman with long silver hair, pulled back into a ponytail, answered the door. She was wearing jeans and a denim shirt. The brown Indian moccasins on her feet didn't make a sound as she walked.

"Get in this house. How have you been?" She hugged Noelle with all her heart. "Who is this fine looking man, Noelle?"

"This is client of mine, Aunt Treena." John looked at her, surprised at the sound of his introduction.

"John, Aunt Treena. Aunt Treena, John."

"Pleased to meet you, John. Glad to have you."

"Thanks for letting us come over. I'm pleased to meet you too."

"What are you doing in this neck of the woods?"

"Treen, do you still have your shop set up and ready to use?"

"I use it almost every day. Made a great piece just this afternoon. You'll have to see it."

"Aunt Treena has a pottery shop. Sometimes I come here, and we paint the pieces she has cast. When we're through, she puts them in the kiln, and we have pottery. Sometimes we keep them; sometimes we give them away."

"Are you saying we are going to paint pottery?"

"You're a sharp one."

"You were right. I haven't ever done anything like this, but I'll be glad to try. I must warn you—I may be a creative writer, but painting is not my forte."

Her aunt led them to the rear of the house. They stepped through a back door, went outside, and took a walkway to another building. It was clear that the detached garage had been converted over to a shop for the woman to dabble in her craft.

Over to one side, there was a large glass cabinet packed full of beautiful ceramics. He was shocked at the detail of each piece. She was, in fact, quite talented.

"Did you do all of these?"

"Yes. Over the course of the years, I've accumulated quite a mess. I need to get rid of a lot of it. It is just hard to let some of the pieces go."

She pulled out a ceramic rabbit to show him. "This one was created for my sister. She had been very ill. Eastertime came, and she was in the hospital. I loved her dearly. She had been sick for so long. I had stayed up there with her many a night, but it was difficult because I had kids to raise. As the months went on, we all grew tired, but I swore my sister would never be alone. I always knew she would have done the same for me. Staying with her was the last thing I would ever be able to do for her.

"My brother stayed with her the night before Easter. Easter morning the nurse called and told us that the family should come to the hospital as quickly as possible. My sister was fading fast.

"When we got there, we immediately noticed a drastic change in my sister's breathing. She was laboring for each breath. After the doctor examined her, he said she could go anytime, but he thought she might live for the next several hours, maybe even for a few days.

"I decided that my own family should go to the Easter celebration that my husband's family had planned. I knew small boys couldn't make it through the entire day at the hospital, and they had been so good to let me take care of my sister that past year or so.

"After a while, my brother decided to take my mother home. I would stay with my sister and keep her company on her last Easter, even if she didn't know I was there. When the nurse came into her room to work with her, she asked me to step into the waiting room.

"I was feeling pretty sorry for myself. I was losing my sister, my family was spending Easter without their mom, and I was just plain old tired.

"Pretty soon a young woman came in and sat down beside me. She was reading the paper so we weren't chatting. I was thinking about myself too much to pay very much attention. Before too long, a man and two young boys came out of the elevator carrying Easter baskets and balloons. The mother's face beamed when she saw them. It made me miss my family even more.

"They all visited for a few minutes, and a nurse came into the waiting area. I thought she was there to tell the family that they could go on back to see their family member. Instead, she pulled a syringe from her pocket and gave the woman an injection. I felt small, and I learned the lesson of a lifetime that day. See, that particular floor of the hospital was only for cancer patients. This young mother had cancer, and she was glowing at the prospect of spending a few hours with her two small boys and husband.

"My sister passed away twenty minutes after midnight, but I have never forgotten the lesson I learned that day. God is good all the time, children. Don't ever forget it. I came home and made this Easter bunny to always remind me that such a wonderful day as Easter isn't about eggs and bunnies. It's not even about our families. It is about Jesus, and it should be a day fit for a King."

John wiped his eyes. He hadn't thought about Easter since he was a young boy.

"Thanks for letting us come tonight, Treen," said Noelle.

"Honey, it is a joy having young people to spend the evening with. Let me get you started. Here are some of the casts I have made up. Just pick one. Noelle, you know where I keep the paint. Remember, the light colors go on before the dark. I'm going to slip into the kitchen and fry up some chicken for supper. You have fun, and I'll come and get you when it's time to eat."

"Thanks, Treen."

"Well, which one do you like?"

"This is amazing, Noelle. I have to admit; it sounds like fun."

"I think I'll paint a picture frame. What about you?"

"I believe I'll pick the motorcycle."

Noelle got out the paint and brushes, and she and John settled into painting.

"How do I do this?" John asked.

Noelle stood behind him. She took his brush, loaded some paint on it, and placed it in his hand. Then ever so tenderly, she placed her hand over his, directing it and guiding it. Her hair fell down next to his face. It smelled like almonds and honey. He wanted to kiss her, but he was afraid. He didn't know if she felt what he was feeling.

As she held onto his fingers, she slowly started stroking the back of his hand. He put down the brush and took her face in his hand. As he stood up, he pulled her in close to him. As he kissed her, she kissed him back.

As tough as it was, he pulled back away from her. He didn't want to move too quickly, scaring her. He didn't want to mess this up.

They continued to paint, but things were never going to be the same.

● ● ●

Dinner was great, but it started getting late. Noelle didn't want them to overstay their welcome so she started their good-byes.

"There's no need to rush off," her aunt assured her.

UNHINGED

"I know, Treen, but it is getting late."

"Well, you come back in about a week, and I'll have your pieces fired and ready for you."

"I'll see you soon. I love you." Noelle hugged her aunt.

"I love you too, child. It was nice to meet you, John. You have Noelle bring you back here anytime."

"Thanks for everything. This has been the best evening I've had in a long time," John answered.

As they walked toward the car, John slid his arm around Noelle's waist. "Tonight was wonderful, Noelle."

"It was fun, wasn't it?"

"I really don't want it to end."

"John, I'm not ready..."

"No, I don't mean that. I just want to spend some more time with you."

Noelle was quiet and didn't respond to what he said. "Are you upset with me?" he asked.

"No, not at all. John, I really want to spend more time with you too."

"Listen, I followed you blindly. Now it's your turn."

"I don't know. I trust me. You make me nervous."

"There's nothing to be nervous about. Let me make a quick phone call."

John made sure Noelle was in the car, and then

125

he stepped back a small distance. She could tell he was giving instructions, but she wasn't sure to whom he was speaking.

"We're all set," John said as he got into the car.

Noelle was still nervous, but she really didn't want to leave him. She had never felt anything this strongly before. She wondered if this was what love felt like.

*Dreams have only one owner at a time.
That's why dreamers are lonely.*

ERMA BOMBECK

9

The car was filled with anticipation as they drove. Noelle was dying to know what was going on.

"Give me a hint."

"Do you have any plans for tomorrow?"

"Just work. Why?"

"Can your assistant handle anything that comes up?"

"Probably better than I can. Are you going to tell me what is going on?"

"You'll see soon enough.

He continued driving east until they reached a small airport. He pulled up next to a relatively empty hanger.

"I want to show you something."

"A plane?"

"Not just a plane, *my* plane."

"You have your own plane?"

"Too much?"

"Slightly."

"Now don't judge too quickly. I have a legitimate reason."

"This should be good."

"I travel a lot. If I can work while I travel, I actually make money."

"So you have your own plane to save money?"

"That sounds so harsh when you say it like that," laughed John.

"Hey, who am I to frown upon your frugal ways?"

As they boarded the plane, John made a phone call. "We're ready."

"What are we ready for?"

"You'll see."

Once inside, he showed her around the spacious cabin. It was done in rich cherrywood and dark leather. It had a masculine feel, but it didn't seem overbearing or hard. It made you want to curl up with a good book and relax.

"Have a seat." They both sat down on a soft leather sofa. She sat a little ways away from him.

"Thank you for letting me see your plane. It's lovely."

"Well, I didn't really bring you here to see the plane."

"Oh?" She got a little nervous. She didn't want things to move too fast.

"Stop worrying! I told you that's not what I have in mind."

"I'm sorry. I'm a little nervous."

She no sooner spoke those words, when she felt movement. The plane was starting to taxi to the runway.

"We're moving!" Noelle was surprised. "Are we going to fly for a while?"

"Sort of."

"This really is fun. When I woke up this morning, I had no idea my day would unfold like this."

"I probably should tell you the rest of the plan."

"The rest? What else could we be doing?"

"We are taking a short trip."

"A short trip? Where to?"

"Las Vegas."

"We are flying to Las Vegas tonight?"

"I know it's late, but I thought you might enjoy a night out."

"I haven't ever been to Vegas."

"Then I have a lot to show you."

"Like what? I don't gamble."

"Great, because I don't either."

"I would like to see some of the hotels. Are they as beautiful as I have heard?"

"They are spectacular."

"Which one will we go to?"

"We are going to several of them. No one can come to Vegas without seeing the typical tourist attractions."

"Are things open tonight?"

"The casinos are open at night, but the things I want to show you will be open tomorrow."

"What will we do until then?"

"I would suggest that we get a little sleep. When we wake up, we'll have a great time."

"Where are we going to sleep?"

"I reserved two rooms at the Luxor."

"The hotel with the pyramid?"

"Yes, it's my favorite."

"Oh no! I didn't bring any clothes or . . ."

"No worrying, I said. The Luxor has several clothing stores, and you will have carte blanche to buy anything you need. There is even a place to buy cosmetics or toiletries or anything else you want. Please charge anything and everything you need to your room."

"Oh, John. I know this is crazy, but it sounds like so much fun!"

"I'm really glad you think so. Hey, do you want to try to catch a nap before we get there?"

"I think I'm just too excited. Do you mind if we talk for a while?"

"Not at all. Tell me something about yourself."

"Like what?"

"How did you decide to get into the publishing business?"

"Actually, I wanted to be a writer."

"A writer? What kind of writer?"

"That's where I hit a snag in my plan. I like so many kinds of books that it was hard for me to decide what to write about. I have several books that I have started, just none that I have finished. Maybe I should write a book called *Fifty Ways to Start a Story*. What do you think?"

"You write it and I'll buy it. I've been rather stuck lately. Maybe I could use that book." John grinned at her.

"Oh, thank you."

"Seriously, I am glad you went into publishing. Otherwise, we would not have ever met."

"Me too."

"What made you start writing, John?"

"You probably won't believe me, but a teacher encouraged me. She taught me how to have style and how to communicate. I liked the positive attention she gave me. I started writing and never looked back. I had an aunt that was an editor for a publishing company, and she got them to look at my work."

"What did you write about?"

"Everything. I wrote a story about a superhero, and I wrote one about a family living on a farm. That one was really good. I think I could cut you a deal on that one."

"What an opportunity for us, but no thanks. Our goal is to make money."

"Ouch!"

As they flew to Vegas, they couldn't stop talking. They shared their hearts with each other. John had never told anyone the things he told Noelle. This was so different from all his other relationships.

When the plane approached Las Vegas, she was amazed at the lights. They looked like a million diamonds tossed in the dark, landing in a magical formation. As they got off the plane, a limo was waiting for them on the airstrip. John asked the driver to take them to the Luxor. It was hard for Noelle to believe that six hours ago she was in the suburbs, painting ceramics.

The car pulled up in front of the large hotel. The lights running up the corners were capped off by the huge light on the top of the pyramid. Stepping out of the car, they made their way down the walkway to the lobby.

When Noelle stepped inside, she couldn't believe it. The Egyptian statues were huge. She had no idea it would be so spectacular. Noelle didn't know much about the Bible, just what Aunt Treena talked to her about when she went to her house to paint. Treena would sit for hours telling her Bible stories. She remembered her aunt Treena telling her about the Israelite slaves in Egypt. God sent Moses to set them free. Looking at these huge figures and grand accessories made her realize how difficult it might have been for Moses to walk away from royalty to join the slaves. Moses was probably used to living in an environment much like this—spectacular and regal. It surely made her appreciate what Moses did.

The hotel had their rooms ready. John had chosen rooms in the pyramid, as close to the top as he could get them. They rode the inclinator up to their respective suites, next door to each other.

The rooms did not disappoint. The bathroom was larger than the one she had at home and was covered in marble. She was getting very tired, and a hot bath sounded wonderful.

When they said goodnight, he reminded her to charge whatever she needed to her room. She would go down in the morning and find something to wear. She closed the door to her room and thought about how lucky she felt.

John went into his room and closed his door. His entire life was different just for knowing Noelle. He had told her his innermost thoughts.

He intended to marry Noelle.

● ● ●

The next morning Noelle awoke about 10 a.m. She threw her clothes on and ran a comb through her hair. The shops and boutiques had been open for a while.

As she walked into one of the clothing boutiques, she asked what they had in her size. There was everything from casual shorts to elegant evening dresses. She wanted to look nice, but she also wanted to be comfortable and wanted to enjoy the day. She picked a pair of khaki pants and a long-sleeved white T-shirt. It looked sporty but nice. She added a pair of brown mules and a few pieces of jewelry. She also bought a few rhinestone hairclips to put her hair in an updo, just in case.

Next she went to a little shop in the hotel and bought toiletries, makeup, and other accessories. Then she hurried up to her room to continue getting ready. At 11:15, she was almost ready to go. A knock on her door made her smile. One final look in the mirror, and she was set.

John stood on the other side, nervous as a schoolboy. He hoped she didn't regret coming to Las Vegas with him.

Her face beamed when she opened the door. He felt himself relax. This hadn't been a mistake. She looked so pretty. Today would be fun.

"Are you ready to see Vegas?"

"Ready! Let me grab my purse."

Closing the door behind her, she stepped forward into her future.

• • •

"Are you hungry?" asked John.

"I'm starving. It has been hours since we ate that fried chicken."

"What are you hungry for?"

"You know, a burger sounds great."

"A burger it is."

He took Noelle to the Harley Davidson Café. They both ordered a burger with slaw on it. When they finished eating, they went upstairs to see Ann-Margret's bike. They had been starving, and the meal couldn't have been better.

Next they headed over to Treasure Island to watch the pirate show. Vegas was a little slow at Christmastime so there wasn't too big of a crowd pressing in on them. The guns went off and the ship burned up and sank, just as it always did. The show was performed for the crowd several times a day, but it was all new to Noelle. It was only a free show, open to the general public, but Noelle felt special watching it.

Noelle wanted to see New York, New York. She was amazed at the detail. The "grates" in the floor put out "steam." The most fun part of the hotel was the roller coaster. It went from the inside of the building to the outside of the building and back in again. They rode it several times, and John felt like a kid again. Noelle wasn't like the other women. She knew how to have fun. She didn't seem to want anything from him. All of a sudden, he remembered the contract. It caused a slight catch in his fun, but he chose to ignore it. He needed to get that handled so he wouldn't be wondering about her intentions.

After they had ridden it as many times as they could stand, they walked outside. Noelle thought Vegas would be decorated for Christmas, but it really wasn't. When she thought about it, she realized Christmas was a Christian holiday. Vegas wasn't exactly known for its Christian lifestyle. However, in front of the hotel, there was a small stage. The dancers came out and danced in their Christmas costumes. The men were in tuxes and the women were in short, red velvet dresses, trimmed with white fur. Noelle loved the white retro go-go boots.

It was getting dark outside. John wanted her to see the eruption at the Mirage at nighttime. Tourists were gathered around waiting on the show. All throughout the day, things had been very platonic between the two of them. It was important to John that Noelle understood his intentions. He knew he had a bad reputation, and he had to repair that image as best he could.

As they stood there waiting, Noelle leaned back against him. He slid his arms around her waist and put his mouth close to her ear.

"Are you glad you came?" John whispered.

"I'm very glad. Are you glad you brought me?"

"Noelle, I couldn't be happier. I had forgotten what happy felt like."

As the volcano erupted, the two felt as one. It was like a silent signal that was meant to be.

"Noelle, I had made arrangements to fly us home tonight."

"Oh, okay."

"However, would you consider staying here with me one more day?"

"I would love to stay here, John."

"I'm so glad. I'll make sure the Luxor extends our reservations. You'll probably need to make another run to the boutique."

"My pleasure." Noelle grinned at John.

"Let's go back to the hotel, and you can get some clothes for tomorrow. While you are looking for something, make sure you grab an outfit for tonight. I have somewhere special to take you."

"What should I get?"

"We're going to a finer restaurant. Nothing too fancy, but it's nice."

Things just kept getting better. She picked out jeans and a sweater for the next day, and the store had a simple but pretty, one-piece black dress. She bought a pair of heels to match, and then she chose a few more pieces of jewelry.

They each went back to their own rooms, agreeing to meet in two hours. Noelle took advantage of the time. She ran a hot bath and enjoyed relaxing. She even fell asleep for about twenty minutes in the tub. Getting out, she dried off with the thick towels and made a cup of coffee. She could use a small pick-me-up.

The dress was becoming on her, and it made her look almost ten pounds lighter. She put her hair up, using the rhinestone bobby pins she had purchased. They added just the right amount of sparkle. The faux pearls completed the ensemble.

Two hours had passed before she knew it. John knocked on her door. When she opened it, she took his breath away. His reaction startled her. "Is this okay?" she asked as she motioned to her outfit.

"I never . . ." He couldn't finish his thought.

"Where to tonight?" She didn't want to embarrass him.

"We are going to a place called the Voodoo Café and Lounge. I thought we would eat at the café. It is on the fiftieth floor of the Rio."

"How exotic!"

"There is something I need to do first."

"What? Do you need to go back to your room?"

"No. I would like to come into your room and sign my contract."

"Now?"

"Noelle, I want our business to be settled. I don't want to continue on in limbo."

"Sure. Jacqui sent a courier to bring a new, clean contract to the hotel. It's lying on my table. Come on in. John, I don't want you to feel pressured to sign this."

"I don't. I just don't want to think about it anymore. I feel so much better than I did. I was so burned out, but now I feel rested and relaxed. I don't want to quit working; I just needed a break."

John leaned over and signed the contract. It was done, all official. "Now let's go."

The limo took them to the Rio to eat at the famous restaurant. The chef did a wonderful job preparing the food, and the atmosphere was dark and romantic. They talked and laughed. When they finished, he took her hand and led her to the fifty-first floor. They walked through the lounge, but didn't stop. He had intentionally set out to show her the lights of Vegas at night.

They walked to the balcony. He thought the night looked enchanted. He didn't know if it was the night or the company he kept, but he knew he didn't want to go back to the same old life he led before.

They ordered two cups of hot coffee and sat down in a darker corner of the balcony. "Are you too chilly?"

"It's a little cool, but not bad. It kind of reminds me of your house."

"I haven't even thought about my house since we left."

"I haven't thought about work. I haven't even thought about Christmas, and tomorrow is Christmas Eve."

"Noelle, may I ask you a question?"

"Sure."

"What do you want from your life?"

"What do you mean?"

"Do you want to expand your career, or do you want marriage?"

"I guess I never thought I would have to choose. I have always wanted both."

John stood up, faced Noelle, and got down on one knee. "Noelle, I want to give you both."

"What?"

"I want to give you both. I want to marry you. I am in love with you."

"Oh, John. I love you too."

"I know it is happening quickly, but I don't ever want to face life without you. Please, marry me."

"I will."

"Oh, Noelle." He sat down next to her and pulled her close to him. The kiss was only the second one they had ever shared. There was something good and true about remaining pure with her. She was worth the effort.

"When can we get married?" he asked.

"Well, a wedding takes awhile to plan."

"What would you think about us getting married in the morning, then flying home? We could spend Christmas at *our* ranch."

"Tomorrow? Wow, that is quick, but it's also exciting, and I don't want to wait."

They left the Voodoo and went back to the Luxor. They went to the food court and sat in a quiet spot. Two hours had passed, and they were still planning their lives. Eventually, they decided to get a good night's sleep so they could enjoy their big day.

After they went to their respective rooms, each stayed awake, staring at the ceiling, believing in their own hearts that they had made the right decision.

Only time would tell, and they weren't letting time have its say.

> *If fear is cultivated*
> *it will become stronger,*
> *if faith is cultivated*
> *it will achieve mastery.*
>
> JOHN PAUL JONES

10

The next morning came early. They chose to keep things simple so they decided to wear their regular street clothes. They could have a huge reception when they returned to the city. Still, they went to a local jewelry store and picked out rings. They felt like a tourist cliché running all over town, working on a wedding. Time seemed to fly by, and before you knew it, it was 4:00 P.M. on Christmas Eve.

    It was exciting, and no one knew about it but them. Since John always had press wherever he went, it was like a miracle. He had let his beard grow out over the last few days, and with a ball cap, he looked like a regular guy. They had taken lots of pictures, and no one had even suspected who they were. Little did they know that their pictures would turn into one of the world's most famous wedding albums.

Their last stop was the chapel. It was quaint, and not a major headliner as far as marriages went. When they walked through the front door, a bell tinkled letting someone know they were there. Out came a young man, presumably a college student.

"Can I help you?" asked the man.

John and Noelle looked at each other, holding hands and smiling. John answered, "Yes. We would love to get married."

"All right. We've got a few things to fill out, and I'll need to call a preacher."

He handed them a legal-looking form and a pen. While they excitedly filled out the paperwork, he made a phone call.

"The preacher will be here in 15 or 20 minutes. You can have a seat."

"Thank you," they both answered.

"Hey, do you want a DVD or flowers or something?"

It was such a plain wedding that the thought of all the extras almost seemed to ruin the magic.

"We're fine. We just want to get married," John answered.

As the almost-married couple took a seat, they looked over their wedding oasis—plain, a little outdated, with one lone vase of plastic flowers sitting on the wedding alter. They didn't say much as they sat there. This definitely didn't seem like the kind of wedding a famous person and his soon-to-be wife would have. Maybe that's why they liked it. It seemed personal. No press. No paparazzi. Just them and their unannounced love. No one could tell them to wait. No one could say, "Have you thought this through?" No one could ruin this moment.

The preacher came in, true to word, in about 20 minutes. She was a black woman, who appeared to be Jamaican. She seemed warm and kind, and yet she was much more serious about the vows that they were making than they had anticipated. Noelle was glad.

As the wedding began, she pronounced each of their names with her native accent. They almost sounded like strangers' names, and John and Noelle did their best not to visibly smile. Yet even through the unusual dialect, she reminded them of what God said about marriage. Much of what she said came from I Corinthians 13. She talked about love being patient and kind, quick to forgive, and never keeping track of wrongs. She told them that this was the kind of love God gave them, and He expected them to give that same kind of love to each other.

Just as she pronounced them husband and wife and gave them permission to kiss, John backed into the only decoration in the room, knocking the vase of flowers to the ground. He quickly picked the vase up, sat it in its designated spot, and then they both burst into laughter.

This was not the wedding Noelle had planned all of her life, but it was a sincere and heartfelt wedding. It was a day filled with joy, hope, and plans for a good life with the man she loved. She turned to him and looked into his dark eyes. "I love you, John Brittingham."

"I love you, Noelle Brittingham."

The chauffer had the car waiting outside. As they drove down the Vegas Strip, they stood up through the moon roof and waved at everyone they passed. For the first time in a long time, John felt at ease and carefree. Being crazy and unpredictable was something he was good at, but he had forgotten how to enjoy it.

• • •

The car continued on to the airport, and as John and Noelle boarded the plane to return home, a young man greeted them. "Good evening, Mr. and Mrs. Brittingham."

"Good evening," John responded.

"May I serve you dinner when you are settled?"

"That would be wonderful. What's on the menu?" Noelle chimed in.

"Beef tips with rice, accompanied by fresh asparagus with hollandaise sauce."

"Wow. Sounds great. Is that okay with you, John?"

"Sure. I just want to enjoy our first meal together."

"I'll set up your table immediately following take off. We should be leaving within the next ten minutes. Dinner will be served in approximately 30 minutes."

"Perfect." John wasn't really listening to the young man. He was staring at Noelle. She looked more beautiful than ever. Her eyes that normally sparkled were absolutely dancing tonight. Her hair was falling slightly over her eyes, but they wouldn't be contained. They reached out and commanded his heart.

Noelle couldn't have been happier. As if being offered the position of senior editor wasn't enough, she had eloped with their new number one author. She wondered what the board members would say about that. She didn't care, not tonight.

Her mind couldn't help but feel uneasy about telling Jacqui. She loved Noelle and wanted the best for her. Noelle knew all too well that Jacqui was going to be disappointed that Noelle had made such a rash decision. What could she tell her? There really wasn't any explanation except—well, love. Surely Jacqui would understand being in love.

Noelle looked over at John as he sat some luggage in the bedroom. He was so handsome, and he had been more kind and gentle than she could ever have imagined. His reputation was unfortunate. She just couldn't believe that side of him existed, although she had seen the photos of him with a different woman every night. At least it seemed that way.

As she thought of some of those pictures, she wondered if he could be happy with only having one woman the rest of his life. Of course, why would he have married her if he hadn't believed in their marriage himself? Noelle felt a little insecure all of a sudden.

"John?"

"Yes, Honey?"

"Do you think we will make it?"

John sat the luggage down and moved in next to her on the sofa. "Why in the world would you ask a question like that?"

"I'm sorry."

"No. Tell me the truth. Why did you ask the question?"

"I feel bad saying this."

"I don't want any secrets, Noelle. I want us to be open and honest."

"Okay. I just want to get this off my chest. After I am finished, I won't bring it up again. I promise."

"Shoot."

"I've seen so many pictures of you with women—all different women, all beautiful women."

"Noelle, I want to be honest with you. You'll just have to trust me on this. Many times my previous publisher insisted that I accompany a new starlet to the meet and greets that they arranged. Half of the time, I didn't even know the girl's name until I picked her up for the event. Now I said I would be honest. This is the part you won't like." John stopped talking and hung his head.

"John, what's the matter?"

"Noelle, my lifestyle used to be fun. I did enjoy going out with all of those women; that's the truth. Yet whether I woke up with one or I didn't wake up with one, I felt empty inside. It's like I had no joy."

"I'm sure you know that I have had relationships too. It was stupid for me to bring this whole thing up."

"No, it wasn't. Tonight is our wedding night. I want to have the slate clean from the very beginning."

"All right. How can we do that?"

It seemed so odd to be talking about these matters now, when they should have been making love. Yet in the rush of things, there were many topics that they hadn't discussed. It would take some time to get to know each other, but they had the rest of their lives.

"My turn for a question," said John.

"Okay..." Noelle answered nervously.

"Have you ever been in love before?"

Noelle sat there for a moment. Her mind automatically rushed to that night in September, over two years ago. Michael had asked her to marry him. She didn't want to lie, but this was their wedding night. Love was kind of an overused word anyway. Besides, she hadn't married Michael.

"Not really, although I have dated someone steady." Noelle knew she was lying, but she felt trapped and pressured. *Why did I start this mess?* she thought to herself. She rapidly decided to take the focus from herself. "What about you?"

"I'm not even sure I had the capability to love before I met you, Noelle."

"Okay, whatever. Stella looked pretty cozy."

"Stella was a mistake. I told you before; I never had a physical relationship with Stella. She stayed in the guesthouse, and I stayed in the main house." John knew he had to make her understand. He put his hands on her shoulders, making her face him directly.

"Noelle, look at me." She looked into his eyes and realized how serious he was. "I never felt like I belonged to anyone. I never felt a woman's heart beat with mine. All I ever did was kill time, and I couldn't regret it any more than I do now."

"Why?"

"Noelle, I would give anything to give you a heart that was untainted, but my heart has had so many pieces taken out of it that, in a way, it is damaged. It is as if every one of my lovers took a tiny piece of me, and I can't have the pieces back. When I met you, I felt as though you had gathered all those pieces in your hands and made them new. I wanted to believe I could be made new—that you would accept me and love me, past and all. You are able to gather my heart and mind and soul and give them back to me in better harmony than I ever had on my own."

"John, I don't know what to say."

"Say you know we'll make it. I have to believe that, Noelle."

"We will make it, John. We just have a lot to learn about each other."

As their lips met in a kiss, the young man came in and announced that dinner was served. With everything out in the open, the air felt better. Noelle was glad they could stop talking so seriously for a while. They enjoyed the great dinner, complete with candlelight and laughter. When the table had been cleared, John asked Noelle if she would like to rest for a while.

"That sounds good. Will you join me?"

"I thought you would never ask."

As the plane settled in for the long flight, John and Noelle settled into their first bed together.

● ● ●

"Maria? Are you home?" John shouted for Maria, but it was already 10 P.M. on Christmas Eve. She wanted to be with her family too.

There was no response. "Well, I guess it is only you and me."

"I'm glad."

As they stood in the kitchen, John took Noelle in his arms. He held her close and slowly kissed her neck. Tonight would be a special night. He took her hand and led her to their bedroom.

This Christmas morning, John would not wake up alone.

*When wealth is lost, nothing is lost;
when health is lost, something is lost;
when character is lost, all is lost.*

BILLY GRAHAM

11

Stella Stone sat at the bar in Phil's Place, looking out the front window, oblivious to Christmas Eve. A BMW pulled up outside, and an expensive suit stepped out. He looked like he needed a shave.

He came in and sat a few stools down from her. Other than the couple in the back booth, they were in the bar by themselves, with only the bartender to keep them company. He ordered a drink and turned around to watch the TV. Stella could tell he was unhappy, and although he looked a little unsettled, Stella warmed right up to him and his BMW.

"Is everything okay?" Stella poured on all of the compassion she could muster.

"I'm fine," he answered. He didn't act as if he realized a beautiful woman was sitting in front of him. He didn't even turn his head. He just kept staring at the TV.

"Is this seat taken?"

He lifted his eyes and saw Stella for the first time. She was pretty. He thought about his wife. She didn't want to spend Christmas with him. He wasn't even sure where she was at, and he was sick and tired of being sick and tired.

"It is now." He pulled the seat out a little, gesturing for Stella to sit down.

"You don't look fine." Stella placed her hand on his back.

He looked at her beautiful, but somewhat sad face. "What's your name?"

"Stella."

"Well, Stella. Why are you in here on Christmas Eve?"

"Geography."

"Geography?"

"Everyone has to be somewhere. Here is as good of place as any."

He stared at her. He didn't know who she was, and he didn't care. His wife had not done right by him. He didn't deserve what had happened. No one should have to be alone at Christmas.

"May I buy you a drink?" the stranger asked.

"I'll take a bourbon and Coke."

"Bourbon and Coke for the lady, please." The

man looked toward the bartender as he placed his order.

"I don't think you ever told me your name," Stella said. He wasn't overly excited about sharing his name. He didn't want to call her later. He just wanted to ease his pain.

"Mike."

"Mike? It's nice to meet you, Mike."

"What are you doing in here? Doesn't a nice guy like you have a wife and kids to spend Christmas with?" She had noticed the ring that he still wore on his finger.

"Apparently, nice guys like me are a dime a dozen. I had a wife and kids, and she decided that there was more to life than being my wife."

"Is there?" He thought about it for a minute. Stella was afraid she had scared him off. "I'm sorry. That is none of my business."

"It doesn't matter. I just can't figure it out. I gave her whatever she wanted, you know. If she wanted to take an art class, I paid for it. If she wanted a bigger house, I paid for it."

"She sounds spoiled." Mike ignored what she said.

"What about you?" Mike changed the subject.

"What about me?"

"You still haven't said why you are here."

Stella looked at him, but she didn't say anything. She took a drink. "You seem like a nice guy. Do you come in here often?"

"Just lately. I don't see much point in sitting at home by myself. I didn't know how hard the holiday would be. I'll be glad when tomorrow's over with."

They had a few more drinks and talked for a couple of hours. He told her about the girl he really loved over two years ago. He had wanted to marry her, but she wasn't ready to be married. After the breakup, he met his wife. They were married within three weeks. Nine months later, she had given birth to twins. Yet somewhere in the chaos, he had actually fallen in love with her and the two doe-eyed girls that called him "Daddy."

Everyone outside the doors of the bar was scurrying from place to place, trying to finish last minute shopping. Time didn't have any meaning in an atmosphere like Phil's Place. Every thought and every word only reflected the moment.

Slowly she took his hand in hers. "It is a lonely time of year." He looked down at his drink. He knew once he crossed this line, he might never be able to go back home. He wanted his wife back, but he was tired of fighting the battle. The second he left the bar with her, he would be stepping out of the timeless and into the eternal. He knew it was wrong, but the drinks had made him complacent. He didn't care anymore, not really.

"Can I give you a ride?" he asked Stella.

"Where are you going?"

"I'm leasing a condo down the road."

Stella got into his BMW, and they headed for his house. Stella knew this wouldn't make her happy. She gave up on happy years ago. It just made her less alone. *What kind of person spends Christmas Eve with a total stranger?* she asked herself. She wasn't sure if this situation reflected more poorly on him or on herself.

When they arrived at his house, he turned on the lights and threw his keys on the table. The condo was nice, but messy. The sports section was spread out on the table, and fast-food boxes were piled on the counter.

"Sorry about the mess. I need to take out the trash."

Stella didn't answer, mostly because she didn't care one way or the other. She took her cigarettes out of her purse. "Mind if I smoke?"

"No. That's fine."

She lit a cigarette and picked up the sports section. "Do you like sports?" Mike asked.

Stella had to laugh to herself just a little. *This guy is an easy mark,* she thought. "I guess you could say that."

"Who's your favorite team?"

"My favorite team is whoever covers the spread."

"Oh."

"Shocked?"

"A little."

"Don't you think nice girls like to gamble?"

"Do they?" Mike replied. Stella turned away and flicked her cigarette ashes into a used paper cup. She ignored his question.

"Do you have anything to drink?" she asked.

"Sure." As Mike fixed drinks, she wondered how much cash he was carrying.

● ● ●

Jacqui stepped inside the sanctuary to celebrate the midnight Lord's Supper. It was dark and the music was playing softly. Her eyes readjusted, focusing on the Christmas decorations. At the very front of the room, a table was set up that held the Lord's Supper. Her mother had always called it Communion. Jacqui smiled when she thought of her. This Christmas her mother was celebrating the birth of the Christ with the Messiah in person. She had passed away last May, and Jacqui missed her. Yet she knew her mother was happy getting to spend Christmas in Heaven, and she knew Heaven was happy to be spending Christmas with her mother.

Before she approached the table, she stopped in a pew to pray. Taking the Lord's Supper wasn't anything she did lightly. From the time she had accepted Christ, her mother had taught her that the Bible clearly warned there would be serious consequences for taking Communion without repentance. She always stopped to ask God for forgiveness, and she made sure she thanked God for allowing Jesus to take the punishment that she deserved.

As she approached the pastor, he smiled and offered to pray with her. She shared a few personal concerns, and then she asked her pastor to pray for Noelle. She knew Noelle had been in Vegas for a day or two at least, but she wasn't sure what was going on or where she was now. However, she knew Noelle was fast approaching a crossroad in her life. She loved Noelle and only wanted God's best for her. She asked the pastor to pray that when Noelle needed God, she would remember to call out to Him.

After they had finished praying, she took the unleavened bread, representing the sinless body that had been broken for her, for all of mankind. Next she took the juice, thanking God for the blood, Christ's blood, which had been shed for her.

She stayed after for a while and continued to pray. Noelle was heavy on Jacqui's heart. Technically, it was Christmas, and Jacqui had much to be thankful for.

• • •

Once Mike started drinking, he didn't want to

stop, and he eventually passed out. It proved quite profitable for Stella.

Stella knew it wasn't right to steal, but wasn't he trying to steal from her? He had wanted something for nothing. He had invited her to his house for sex, if the truth were to be told. He didn't even know her last name. She was just doing unto him before he had a chance to do unto her. She was no guiltier than he was; at least that's what she told herself. Fortunately, she didn't have to fulfill her end of the bargain. He had been too drunk.

Once he passed out, she was able to look around the condo a little. He had some money in his nightstand as well as his wallet. In the medicine cabinet, she found some newly prescribed Valium, which she stuck in her purse. She left everything else in place. She didn't want the police to be able to trace anything back to her so taking anything to pawn was out of the question.

When she was finished working, she called her friend, Billy, to pick her up. She was drunk and her head was starting to spin. As she stepped inside of his car, she handed him twenty bucks.

"Thanks for coming to get me, Billy."

"No problem. You don't have to pay me, Stell."

"I guess I've got the Christmas spirit. Keep it."

He pulled up to her house and decided he

had better make sure she could get in the door. "You gonna be okay, Stell?" He walked her to the couch.

"I always am, Billy. I'll call you later." Billy reached for the doorknob to leave. "Hey, Billy?"

"Yeah?"

"Can you stay here tonight?"

"I can't, Stell. I've got to get home to my wife. I had to lie to get out tonight. I told her the door was unlocked at the shop. She's probably fuming because I have been gone so long." Stella slumped down and closed her eyes. "Merry Christmas, Stell."

She didn't answer; she was already passed out.

● ● ●

The sun came up, and the snow came down. Noelle awoke, as happy as she had been in years. She looked over at John, who was fast asleep. Silently, she slid out of the bed, tiptoed into the restroom, and found John's robe hanging behind the door. It was a rich navy blue, and it helped to knock off the morning chill.

When she came to visit the first time, she had not toured John's home. They had sat outside, and she hadn't really been much past the entryway. When they came in last night, she saw her new kitchen for the first time. A cup of coffee sounded great. Maybe she would be able to find her way back without waking up John.

She remembered passing through the great room, and so she headed that direction. She could see the sun pouring in through the big, bay window in the dining area. It was the odd kind of winter day that looked warm, even though it was snowing heavily.

Noelle poked around in the cabinets until she found a cup. There was a coffee canister sitting on the hutch. She got some coffee going and decided to wake up her new husband with breakfast in bed. Looking in the refrigerator, she had to smile. There were plenty of eggs, bacon, and sausage, and several cans of biscuits were in the door.

Noelle had worked hard for the last few years, and she normally didn't have time to cook. This would be a nice change of pace. It would be their first Christmas dinner together, but it would be breakfast instead of dinner—and it would be bacon and eggs, not turkey or ham.

As the smell of the bacon drifted into the bedroom, John woke up and saw his wife had beaten him up out of bed. He smiled at the thought of her cooking breakfast. His house felt like a home, not just a house with an office. He got up, slipped on some running shorts and a T-shirt, and went into the kitchen.

She didn't know he was there at first. He loved watching her. She looked even more beautiful in his robe with her hair slightly messy. He thought about the night before.

As she cooked, she was singing a Christmas song to herself. This was the best Christmas he could ever remember.

"Good morning." John startled Noelle as he spoke.

"You scared me! I didn't know you were up."

"You don't have to fix breakfast."

"I want to, John. This is our first meal in our new home. Well, my new home anyway."

John came up and stood behind her as she poured the coffee. She sat the cups down and turned to face him.

"Are you glad you are here, Noelle?"

"I am. Are you glad I'm here?"

"I've never been happier." He leaned over and kissed her, untying her robe. "Let's skip breakfast and go back to bed for a while."

"Breakfast is about done. I'll turn it off, and we can eat it a little later."

They left the eggs in the pan and let their coffee get cold.

● ● ●

Later that morning, John shaved while Noelle took a shower, and then they went into the kitchen to finish breakfast. John had some shorts and a T-shirt that Noelle borrowed until she could move her things over to her new home.

"I'm starved!" Noelle said.

"Me too. Aren't you ever going to feed me, Wife?"

Noelle laughed and hit at him. "I tried, remember?"

"I guess you did. Okay, you're forgiven."

They sat at the big, wooden table and made plans for their future together. There was so much to talk about. It almost didn't seem like Christmas Day. They didn't have gifts for each other, and they hadn't even thought about it.

● ● ●

John and Noelle put on their clothes and headed to the city so Noelle could pick up a few things. There wasn't much traffic since it was Christmas Day.

The doorman greeted her as usual. "Good afternoon, Ms. Reynolds."

"Guess what, Stan. It's Mrs. Brittingham now!"

"Well, congrats to you and the mister. Merry Christmas, Mrs. Brittingham."

"Merry Christmas, Stan."

They entered her apartment. It almost seemed as if she had never lived there. It didn't feel like her home. It felt like a hotel room.

"Make yourself at home," Noelle told John.

"This is so strange. My wife has a home I have never even been inside before. It's kind of a strange feeling."

"That's how I felt last night. I'm not sure I can even find your office again."

John smiled. "We're both going to have a lot of adjustments to make, I'm sure."

"What do you think everyone is going to say?"

"Some will be happy for us. Others will think we're crazy. The press will have a field day so you need to be prepared."

"What's this?" John held up a photo in a silver frame.

Noelle wished she had come up to the penthouse alone. It was an old picture of Michael and her that she hadn't ever taken down from the fireplace.

"Oh, it's nothing. Just an old picture of a friend."

"He doesn't look like 'just a friend.'"

"Hey, let's get my stuff and get out of here. The past is the past, and I want to celebrate our future."

John sat the picture down. He had asked Noelle point blank if she had ever been in love, and she had said no. She looked happy in the picture, very happy. His heart had an uneasy feeling, but he didn't want to borrow trouble. Today was supposed to be a good day. He was on his honeymoon.

Noelle packed a bag as quickly she could, changed into her regular clothes, and grabbed her notebook that she used at home. Having her own things would help break up some of the tension, and maybe she could even get a little work done later on her computer. She had quite a bit to catch up on.

It didn't take her long to get ready. Hanging out at the penthouse wasn't going to help her. She had spent her entire life hoping for the man of her dreams to come along, and John was that man. Even if she felt something for Michael, it was nothing compared to the feelings she had for John. She really hadn't been in love before. She had answered him honestly, but Michael had loved her. That wasn't her fault. This was a new life and a new start.

She closed the door to her penthouse, and she closed the door to her old life.

● ● ●

Stella woke up with a headache, and her mouth tasted like stale cigarettes. *Merry Christmas to me*, thought Stella.

She got up to use the bathroom and looked in the mirror. Her face looked old and tired. She knew she would have to take better care of herself, or she wouldn't be able to make any money. Since she had cut her ties with Molly Red, she hadn't worked over the last week or so.

Stella thought about Molly. What a joke that whole thing had been. If it hadn't been for that stupid and overachieving Noelle Reynolds, she would have been spending Christmas with John Brittingham. She thought about the day she left his ranch.

John hadn't acted as if he hated her. He just seemed to be uninterested in her. Men like John didn't spend much time alone. If he didn't want her, then he wanted someone else.

There was only one way to find out. Stella was going back to John's place. After all, it was Christmas. Holidays could test anyone's desires. If he was by himself, then he might be lonely enough to let her back in. If not, she would find out for sure if her problem was Noelle.

She took a hot bath and soaked for a while, then fixed her hair and makeup. She put on a simple but sporty running suit that made her look younger.

Stella had never had a man turn her down. All men had weaknesses, and Stella was a professional at revealing those weaknesses. Normally, Stella was gone before the man ever knew what hit him.

John Brittingham had been different, although he hadn't started out that way. He had been on the hunt just like all the others.

As Stella dwelled on what happened, she became angry—and then her anger turned to hate. Noelle was the kind of woman who always got the man. Stella had seen him first, and Noelle should have left him alone. Women like her needed to be taught a lesson. Noelle needed to see what it was like to fight for something or someone she wanted. *Let's see how charming and sweet she acts when I get through with her,* Stella vowed.

Stella took the DVD she had secretly made of John and put it in the player. She watched in amazement. With John's back to the camera most of the time, it looked as though he was trying to seduce her. *I wonder what Noelle Reynolds would think if she saw this?* Stella thought to herself. *In fact, maybe she needs to see what John Brittingham is really like.*

She put the DVD in a sack and tied it up with some red string. It almost looked like a real gift. Stella put on her coat, hopped into her car, and put the gift in her purse.

As she headed for John's ranch, she knew it was time to make things right.

● ● ●

When John and Noelle pulled up at the ranch, the snow had started falling again. It was a beautiful white Christmas. John opened the door for Noelle and let her in the house, and then he unloaded the car. Noelle looked around her new great room. The leather furniture was luxurious. The light fixtures looked like real antlers, and there were exquisite furs on the floor, which were used as rugs.

"I think that's about it." John had finished carrying Noelle's bags inside.

"Thanks, Honey. I'll find a spot for these things in the bedroom."

"Move anything you need to."

"Sounds good." Noelle went toward the bedroom, and John went in the kitchen to make a pot of coffee.

Noelle hung up the few things she had hurriedly grabbed at the apartment and went back into the great room where John was sitting. The coffee smelled great.

"How about a cup of coffee?" John offered.

"I would love one." John started to get up, but Noelle stopped him. "I'll get it. If I'm going to make this my home, I need to get use to everything. I need to pick out my favorite cup." Noelle grinned at him.

It took her a minute to find a cup, but in no time, she was back in the great room with John. "This coffee's good. What kind is it?"

"Thanks. The beans are from Hawaii."

"Of course they are."

"What does that mean?"

"Is there anything plain and normal about you? You just seem larger than life."

"Oh, I'm pretty plain and normal," John responded.

"You're pretty anyway." Noelle was proud of her husband. He was a beautiful man to look at, and he had a sweet spirit. He made her feel safe and secure. He didn't seem as though anything bothered him.

"Speaking of pretty, you looked pretty in the picture I saw at your penthouse."

"Oh, John. Let's not talk about it."

"Noelle, I have to know."

"I told you. He was a friend."

"Noelle, I have been with women before. That isn't a secret, but I never gave my heart away. I need to know your heart is mine."

"John, I love you, and things are going to be difficult at times. Because you have been with other women, there is part of me that is concerned about trusting you. How do I know you won't be tired of me six months from now?"

"Noelle, you will always hold my heart. I've told you that before. Those women didn't mean anything to me."

"But Stella lived with you. How can you say that?"

"Stella lived in the guesthouse. There was nothing else to it."

With each of the newlyweds preoccupied, no

one had time to notice the quiet visitor who was listening in silence to their every word.

"Besides, I believe we were talking about you. Remember?"

"Look, I had a friend a few years back whom I dated. He was someone to have dinner with and go to the movie with, but I'm with you now."

John didn't think she was telling the complete truth, but he let it go. "I love you, Noelle."

"I love you too. John, I truly am glad that we are married." He kissed her, and their souls seemed to touch.

"Hey, let's build a fire outside and enjoy the rest of our Christmas Day. We'll take our coffee outside, under the canopy."

"That sounds romantic. I'll get our coats." They walked to the door, opened it, and changed their destinies forever.

A ruffled mind makes a restless pillow.

CHARLOTTE BRONTE

12

Stella had been careful to write down the code for John's gate before she moved out. She wondered why he hadn't changed it after he asked her to leave. It was almost as if he secretly wanted to see her; at least that is what she had told herself when she pulled in through the gate.

She parked the car a short distance from the house. Stella wasn't one to tip her hand too early. She walked the rest of the distance to the door, but decided not to ring the bell. From the side windows on the door, Stella could see inside John's house. He appeared to be home. She stepped back off the porch and went to one of the windows in the rear of the house.

She was shocked at what she saw. It was her! She was moving in! *It should have been me,* she fumed to herself. *That conniving little twit! She stooped even lower than I did. She must have really needed him to sign that contract with her company. Even I wouldn't move in with a total stranger unless there was something in it for me.*

Stella kept watching. She checked the back door to the sunroom. It was unlocked; she slid in unnoticed. She could hear voices, and she heard her name. As Stella heard John say there was nothing to their relationship, she locked her nerves as if they were steel. There was no turning back.

How dare he say that? He certainly acted interested at the bookstore and at the Bistro that night. *And little Miss Noelle?* She made Stella the angriest of all. She had hired Stella to trick John, and now she had wormed her way into his bedroom. *I wonder what John would think if he knew the truth about his little girlfriend?*

Just then, Stella heard the truth. John and Noelle were married. That was unforgivable. *How could that have happened so quickly?* she asked herself.

It was over. Stella was finished with both of them, and she decided to leave the newlyweds a little gift. She went to the front of the house and sat the package containing the DVD on the step in front of the door. The snow fell silently and quickly, covering her tracks as she walked back to her car and drove to her empty house.

After all, what did Santa usually bring naughty boys and girls?

● ● ●

"Are you ready?" John asked Noelle.

"Sure. Will it take long for the fire to get going?"

"Just a minute. All I have to do is push the button." John picked up the coffees, and Noelle opened the door.

As she went outside, she almost stepped on the package. She bent over and picked it up. "What's this?"

"I don't know. Probably just a Christmas gift from a fan."

"You've got to be kidding me."

"I have the gates locked. She must have climbed the fence."

"John, this scares me a little."

"There's nothing to worry about. I'm sure she is long gone."

"I hope so. It's kind of creepy."

"You'll get used to it."

John took the package and threw it on the table in the entry hall. They went outside and had the best Christmas ever.

As they sat and talked, they realized how much

was left to discuss. "I haven't even asked you what your book is about."

John looked at her and laughed. "That's right. You bought a book that you know nothing about. That should send you right to the top of the corporate ladder."

"Laugh now. All they will care about is you."

"I *am* a catch." John grinned at Noelle.

Noelle rolled her eyes and smiled. "Okay. Tell me what I got for my money."

"*It's Top Secret.*"

"Yeah, right."

"I'm not kidding."

"You mean you are not even going to tell me? I'm your wife!"

"No, no, no. That's the name of the book, *It's Top Secret.*"

"Oh. What's it about?"

"It's about a writer who loses his heart to a book publisher. It should be a big hit."

"All right. Don't tell me. I don't care." She turned her back toward him and sipped her coffee.

"I'll tell you. It's about two authors who start to research a book, and they come across a top secret document."

"That actually sounds pretty good."

"Thanks, I try."

"You know what I mean."

"I know what you mean. You think you can make some money off of it."

"Don't take this wrong, because you are a good writer, but it wouldn't matter what you wrote about. It would sell."

"True. However, if I have a book that is mediocre, the next book is less likely to sell. Besides, I make more money from selling movie rights than I make on book sales anyway."

"Then why was picking a publisher such a big deal?"

"I have to be careful. For many years, I have had relationships with people who surprise me everyday—and not in a good way."

"What do you mean?"

"It just seems like everyone wants a piece of me. Some want my time. Some want my endorsement. Some want a photo op. Some want money. Everyone wants something."

"No wonder you wouldn't see me when I called."

"I didn't know you from Adam. The number I give as a contact number is actually answered by a service. They sort through the messages and give me the important ones."

"Would I be on the 'To Call' list now?"

"Mrs. Brittingham, you are number one on the list."

"Why, thank you. Hey, I'm getting a little chilly. Want to go back inside?"

"That's fine." They gathered their cups and headed back into the house. As Noelle walked by the table, she picked up the package.

"Do you want to open it?" Noelle asked John.

"I know it's going to be something ridiculous. Someone wants me to look at his book, or someone wants me to endorse something."

"Maybe not. Maybe it is a Christmas gift for you because the person is such a big fan."

"Hmm. Okay, I give. I honestly don't care anything about it, but you can open it, if you want."

"Good. I'm dying to know what it is." John rolled his eyes, but he had to smile. She seemed like a little girl opening a present from Santa.

Carefully and methodically, Noelle untied the ribbon on the gift bag. When she peeked in, she saw a plain DVD case. It was more like something a homemade DVD would be in. She pulled it out of the bag. There were no markings or labels on it.

"This is weird," Noelle said.

"Told you. It always is."

"Let's play it."

"Maybe I should just call you Pandora."

"Aren't you curious?"

"Not really."

"I am." John looked at Noelle. He could not

refuse her anything. She held his heart in her delicate hands.

"Okay. I can tell that you are never going to be satisfied until you see it. I'll put it in the player."

"Maybe I should make some popcorn," Noelle joked.

"Oh, yes. That would make whatever this is just that much better."

John walked to the player, got the remote, and the two snuggled down on the sofa. The first scene to come up on the screen looked like the very room in which they were sitting.

"This *is* weird," John commented.

"John, I'm not liking this. Why would someone have film of the inside of your home?"

"I don't know."

After a few minutes, John showed up on the screen, followed closely by Stella. John turned off the DVD. "Noelle, we need to turn this off."

"Do you think Stella was here today?"

"I don't know how else something like this would have gotten on my porch."

"Do you think she could see us? Do you think she was watching us?"

"I don't know."

"I want to see it."

"No, Noelle. I don't know how she filmed us, but she never had permission."

"So? What could be so bad?"

"I don't want to find out."

"Don't be ridiculous."

"Noelle, I really don't want to watch it. Please. Do you mind? Today is really important to me. It is our first Christmas together, and I don't want her to be part of it. I don't even want to think about her."

Noelle slumped back onto the sofa. "All right."

"Don't be mad."

"I'm not mad, just curious. If it were me, you would want to see it."

"Look, Stella probably has no idea we are married."

"So?"

"What if this is her 'true love' confession? She would be embarrassed."

"Oh, so now you are watching out for Stella and her feelings?"

"I didn't say that. You're putting words in my mouth, Noelle."

"Am I? Either you are hiding something, or you still care for Stella."

"Good grief! How did you come up with all that?"

"Well, when you try to hide things from me, it makes me suspicious."

"I'm not hiding anything! I didn't even know

what it was! You are the one who insisted on opening it!"

"Then play it. Turn it on and play it!"

"No! Why can't you just be happy that we are together? Why do you want to see what some alcoholic, desperate, crazy lady has to say? What good will come from it?"

"Maybe none, but you should be curious too. Why was she filming you?"

"Because she is crazy, Noelle!" John stood up, and Noelle could feel the anger pressing in around them. They were both angry. He walked to the DVD player, took out the disk, and put it back in its case. Then in one large gesture, he threw the case and headed toward his office.

"That's great, John. We haven't even been married a day!" Noelle screamed.

John kept walking and Noelle sat there, furious and appalled all at once. Why would he try to keep her from seeing something? She looked over on the floor where the case had landed. She stood up and walked to the hall that led to John's office. She didn't see him. She picked up the case, went to the bedroom, and slid the case into her computer bag.

A few hours had passed, and it was getting late. She decided to go check on John. When she rounded the corner to go to his office, they ran right into each other.

"Noelle, I am so sorry."

"No. I'm sorry. It is none of my business."

"Everything is your business if it involves me. I was just being stupid."

"Let's forget it, okay?"

"Sounds good. I'm about ready for bed. Are you tired?"

"It seems like we have been up forever."

"Then let's call it a night, Mrs. Brittingham."

Just as quickly as the fight had begun, it ended. They went back to their bedroom, holding hands and walking closely together.

The night was drawing to a wondrous close, and all was right in the house—almost.

● ● ●

As John lay there fast asleep, Noelle slid out of bed. She hadn't been able to get Stella off her mind. There had to be more to this. She grabbed her computer bag and went into the great room.

Very discreetly, she started her computer and put the DVD into the player. She kept listening for John, but all she could hear was his breathing.

As the DVD started, she watched the screen as John and Stella entered the room. She adjusted the sound, but there didn't seem to be any. Then she saw it all. Stella unbuttoning her blouse. John turning around, putting his hands on her hips, and clearly bending down to kiss her.

He lied! No wonder he didn't want me to see this. Noelle took the DVD out of the player, put it back in its case, and sat it in John's chair.

She had made a mistake. This whole thing was a mistake. What in the world had she been thinking? She didn't know this man, not really. Actually, she did know him, but she had created an image of him that wasn't real. He had made a fool out of her.

He claimed he never even kissed Stella, and nothing physical had happened. *What a fool! I'm not staying here another night,* she told herself.

She was embarrassed and mad and hurt. She didn't even want to see him again, ever. He got what he wanted. He conquered this conquest. This bored playboy had reached an all-time low, and his little reindeer games were nothing but attempts to bring some interest to his blasé life.

He probably intended on divorcing her as soon as the holiday was over. In fact, he might even be planning to get the entire marriage annulled.

She tiptoed into the bedroom and gathered a few things. When she finished, she went back into the great room, took her cell phone from her purse, and called a taxi to come and get her.

She waited about twenty minutes, bundled up in her heavy coat, took what she could carry, and started walking to the gate. She needed to make sure she was there when the taxi arrived so the driver didn't buzz the house.

It was really cold outside. The snow had quit falling, and the wind was whipping through the pine trees. What had seemed peaceful and serene earlier in the day just seemed harsh and foreboding now.

Fortunately, she only had to stand there a few moments before the taxi pulled up. She got in the car, collapsed into the seat, and wept. The driver didn't know what to say so he just asked her where she needed to go.

"Home. Just take me back home."

• • •

It was very late when Noelle unlocked the door to the penthouse. It felt as though she didn't live in either place. She didn't belong anywhere anymore. She was lost and couldn't find her way back.

She dropped everything inside the door and practically fell on the sofa sobbing. Everything was messed up. Her heart was shattered into pieces. Her stomach ached and her eyes were pounding against her head. She was chilled and tired and achy.

As the night wore on, Noelle wore out. With the few pieces of heart she had, Noelle believed that her life would never be good again.

She fell asleep, and visions of Stella danced in her head.

A wounded deer leaps the highest.

EMILY DICKINSON

13

Jacqui had enjoyed her Christmas holiday, but getting back to work felt great. She hated being behind, and she was bound to start out the day with plenty of phone calls and e-mails to return. Since Noelle had taken over, Jacqui had more responsibility. It was a good feeling though. She liked her job and looked forward to the different challenges and opportunities that each day presented.

She hadn't heard from Noelle since she left the office that night with John, except for the voice mail she left saying she wouldn't be back until after Christmas and asking her to send the new contract to the Luxor. It also had led her to believe that she would be in today.

The morning was slipping away. Even if Noelle was running late, which she normally did, she was at the office by 9:15 in the morning. It was 10:45, and there was no word from her. Jacqui decided that she would try her cell phone. No answer.

Jacqui wondered if she misunderstood. She said she would be back after Christmas, but she didn't say exactly which day. Jacqui worked all day with no contact from Noelle.

Something didn't feel right.

● ● ●

John woke up to the sun shining in his window. He looked over and saw that Noelle was already up. As he slipped into his robe, he noticed that something seemed out of place.

The house seemed unusually still. He didn't hear pots or pans clanking around. He didn't smell any coffee brewing. As he moved to the great room, he realized most of her things were gone.

John yelled Noelle's name, but he knew it was futile. He felt an emptiness in the house, in his heart. Everything seemed fine after they made up last night. *Why would she leave?* he asked himself.

Then he saw it. There sat the DVD. *I'll kill Stella for doing this to me!*

He put the disk into the DVD player. He realized how it must have looked to Noelle. He had promised her that nothing happened between Stella and himself, but this DVD made him look guilty.

John picked up the phone and tried to call Noelle's apartment. No answer. In fact, there was no answer on her direct line at work either. The only thing he could do was to go to her and try to convince her to come home.

He got dressed and tried calling her numbers again. Still no luck.

The roads were a little slick from the packed-down snow, but nothing could have stopped him from going to find her.

Whether it was love for Noelle or hate for Stella, he had never made it into the city so quickly.

He had two women to see.

● ● ●

Noelle eventually woke up. She was physically drained and emotionally beaten up. She started crying at the thought of John. She wanted to stop, but it didn't seem possible. She had really fallen for him, and she couldn't imagine having a life without him.

He was everything she was not, both good and bad. He was daring, but reckless. He said things to her that she had longed for a lifetime to hear from a man, but he was a liar.

She looked around her penthouse. It was funny. This was an elegant suite, and she had led an elegant life, until now.

Back home, her grandmother had lived in

a four-bedroom farmhouse. She had passed away years before, and no one had ever moved into the old homestead. Throughout the years, the windows on the old house had eventually been broken out and the shutters had slipped. The door had even come off its hinges and could no longer keep the harsh elements from coming in the once warm and loving home.

That was how Noelle felt. Unhinged. There was nothing protecting her heart. All the harshness of the world had come inside and evicted the love and warmth that had once lived there. The only thing left was the damaged frame of a woman.

The phone rang, but no one was left to hear it.

● ● ●

Jacqui was unsettled about Noelle. She really thought she would be in the office today. She had called her house and her cell phone, and there was still no answer.

She didn't want to overstep her position with Noelle, but she did care about her. This wasn't like Noelle. She was a little disorganized, but she was incredibly responsible.

Jacqui thought of all the places that Noelle could be. There would be no reason for her to be with John Brittingham. Maybe she was with Michael. She had never really gotten over him. She had almost married him.

Jacqui went home that night, and before she went to sleep, she lifted Noelle up in prayer, just as she did each and every night. Wherever Noelle was, God was watching over her.

● ● ●

John stopped at Phil's Place to get some change and use the phone. Noelle hadn't answered her phone all day, and he had gone to her apartment twice, to no avail. Maybe if she didn't recognize the number, she would pick up.

He tried to call. No answer. He sat down and ordered a coffee.

"Do I know you?" the man on the next barstool asked.

"Fairmont High School, class of '92," John bluffed.

"No, I don't know anyone from Fairmont. You look really familiar."

"Maybe I just have one of those faces that looks like everyone else."

"Maybe. Mike Tiner." John actually thought Mike looked familiar, but he didn't say anything.

"Hello, Mike. I'm John."

"Nice to meet you, John. What brings you in here the day after Christmas?"

"I actually just came in to use the phone."

"I see."

John didn't know why, but he felt like talking. "No, my wife left me."

"Go figure. So did mine."

"When?" John asked.

"December 18."

"Right before Christmas?"

"Yep. What about you?"

"Christmas Day."

"Christmas Day? Wow, they say holidays are rough, but Christmas Day?"

"Actually it was Christmas night. I went to bed, and when I woke up, she was gone."

"What did you do?"

"I've tried to call her. I've tried to see her, and nothing. She is nowhere to be found," John said.

"Good night! What in the world did you do?"

"That's just it. I didn't *do* anything."

"Whatever you say."

"Okay, I did something stupid a few weeks ago, and that something is coming back to bite me."

Mike laughed. "Was the something that got you in trouble a blonde or a brunette?"

John shook his head. "She was a blonde, but it's not how it sounds."

"This ought to be good."

"Let me explain. I was working one night. All of sudden, standing in front of me is a beautiful, drop-dead woman. You know the kind—the kind you wait a lifetime to meet."

Mike nods. "Go on."

"Well, I ask her out, and she meets me when I get off work."

"You didn't think this would be a problem for your wife?"

"That's just it. I didn't have a wife then."

"I thought you just met her a few weeks ago."

"I know. It sounds bad."

"Go on."

"Anyway, to make a long story short, I liked this woman, and I had hopes of getting to know her better. So I invited her out again."

"Still no wife in the picture?"

"Still no wife. As I got to know her, I found out she was having her house remodeled and was living in a hotel temporarily. Since I have a guesthouse, I asked her to move in."

"Ouch."

"No kidding. It was nothing but painful. She was nothing as she seemed."

"I feel your pain, brother."

"Anyway, she has caused trouble ever since."

"So how does a wife fit into this mess?"

"Oh, the story is too long. Why are you here?" John actually wanted to know. Taking the focus off his problems felt somewhat relaxing.

"Talk about a long story. It actually began with the woman before my wife, over two years ago."

"You were still in love with someone from your past?"

"Yeah, I guess I was, but that all changed. I truly love my wife now."

"Your old flame must have been some kind of woman to make you remember her so passionately," John said.

"She was an amazing woman, John, and when she looked at you, her eyes bore into your soul."

"Really?"

"You couldn't understand."

"I might understand better than you think."

"Anyway, we were in love, and then she left me. I met my wife on the rebound."

"Did she know about the other woman when you met?"

"Everything. I didn't want to keep secrets, except for one thing. I didn't tell my wife that I had asked her to marry me. I thought just telling her about the woman would be enough. I was wrong."

"She found out?"

"Oh, yeah. Anyway, now I've really messed up."

"What do you mean?"

"I met someone the other night. I had too much to drink, and I honestly don't know what happened.

She was gone the next morning when I woke up. My money was missing too."

"Were you able to get it back?"

"I don't know where she lives. I have been coming in here because I keep hoping to see her again."

"Any luck?"

"No."

"Well, I wish you luck, Mike."

"Thanks, John." The cold air hit John in the face as he opened the door to try Noelle's penthouse one last time.

At this rate, he would be a bachelor by New Year's Eve.

● ● ●

Stella went back to her house that afternoon feeling vindicated and proud. She had given them what they deserved. These types of people, who were used to having everything, needed to be brought down a notch, and she was just the person to do it.

That Noelle Reynolds had her nerve. She hired her to trick John Brittingham, and then had her fired because she wasn't doing it fast enough. She probably wasn't even going to stay with him once he signed the contract.

I wonder what he would think if he knew about her little plan? Stella thought. Maybe it was time to pay Mr. Brittingham another visit.

And she would, just as soon as she had a drink.

● ● ●

Noelle didn't even realize until evening that she was supposed to go to work. She didn't even want to think about work. Maybe she would never go back.

After all, what was she going to do now? She didn't ever want to see John again. How would she ever be able to work with him?

Jacqui was going to be disappointed in her. *Jacqui,* she thought to herself, *this would never have happened to Jacqui.* Jacqui didn't let herself get into situations like this. Jacqui didn't marry men she didn't know, especially men with wicked reputations.

Jacqui hadn't even wanted Noelle to go out with John. How would she ever explain marrying him? Maybe she wouldn't. Maybe she wouldn't tell anyone. Maybe John was getting the marriage annulled at this very minute. Maybe ...

Noelle spent the entire day on the sofa, except when she was in bed, crying . She finally got up long enough to make some coffee. She looked as bad as she felt. Her hair was undone, and she hadn't had a bath since the day before. Her teeth weren't brushed, and she still had on what was left of yesterday's makeup.

On her way to the bathroom, she heard the doorbell. She looked at the clock. It was 11:30 P.M.

Who could it be at this hour? she asked herself.

Her heart raced faster. What if it was John? Unlikely. He was probably glad she left. It had all been a joke to him anyway. She was nothing more than a prize for a schoolboy prank.

She didn't want to see anyone, not tonight, not ever. Maybe it was time to move back home. At least there she knew what people really thought, and no one wanted to use her just for the fun of it.

She went to the restroom, and then went to the kitchen to get some coffee. She had never turned on the pot. Nothing was going to go right for her. She turned off the kitchen light and went back to bed.

She had cried all of the tears she could cry. Tomorrow was a workday.

She rolled over and didn't set the clock.

● ● ●

The next day when Jacqui arrived at the office, John Brittingham was sitting there, waiting.

"Hello. You're Jacqui, right?"

"Yes, Mr. Brittingham."

"Call me John."

"Okay, John. What can I do for you?"

"I need to see Noelle."

"Well, she's not in yet. She normally doesn't come in until about 9:15 or so. Do you want to leave a message?"

"No. I would like to wait, if that's okay?"

"That's fine." Jacqui really didn't want him to wait. When Noelle did come in, she would be behind and would not want to mess with this guy first thing before she even took off her coat. Jacqui really wished he would set an appointment and then leave. However, that wasn't going to happen.

"If you don't mind, I'll let you wait in the conference room," Jacqui offered.

"That's fine."

"Would you like some coffee?"

"Coffee sounds great. Black."

"I'll get it. Do you need anything else?"

"Jacqui, did Noelle say anything to you about me?"

"What do you mean?"

"Since she's been back in town."

"I haven't spoken to Noelle since two days before Christmas. She just said she was going on a mini-Christmas vacation."

"Oh. Okay."

"Why did you ask me about Noelle?"

"It's just that . . ."

"It's just what?"

"Never mind."

Jacqui looked at him suspiciously. He knew something that he wasn't telling. She backed away from him and went to get the coffee. She was getting seriously worried about Noelle, and she didn't trust this man. She hadn't seen Noelle since she left with him that evening after work.

When she returned with the coffee, John was making a call on his cell phone. She intentionally waited to see whom he was trying to call. However, he hung up without waiting for his connection to go through.

"Thank you," John said.

"You're welcome."

"So you haven't had any word at all from Noelle?"

"No. Like I said, she took a small trip over the holiday." Now Jacqui was anxious to get out of the room. She didn't feel right talking to John Brittingham about Noelle. Noelle's personal life was none of his business.

Jacqui excused herself and went back to her desk. It was getting late. Noelle should have already been at work. John seemed nervous and a little rattled. Why was he so insistent on waiting for her?

Jacqui kept wishing Noelle would walk through the door. She checked the clock. It had passed 9:15 almost twenty minutes ago. She kept trying Noelle's cell phone and her home number. After she left what seemed like the tenth message, she gave up. She had to go back in and face John.

He looked at her anxiously when she entered

the conference room. "Is she here?" John asked, as he stood to his feet.

"No. I'm afraid not. She may have stopped to run an errand on her way in. Would you like to leave her a message or set up an appointment?"

"I really need to see her."

"I'm sorry. I just don't know what to tell you."

"May I wait for a while longer?"

"If you wish."

"Jacqui, please don't be upset with me. I don't know what else to do either."

"No problem."

John sat back down, Jacqui went back to her desk, and the clock kept ticking.

● ● ●

Stella had intended to go back out to John's, but she drank too much. She fell asleep without getting anything accomplished.

When she awoke the next day, she had a hangover. It didn't take much to put her in a bad mood. She had a rather unrealistic view of what was going on, but her own reality was all that mattered to her.

She made some strong coffee and forced herself to get cleaned up. Her bitterness was driving her to keep going. She wouldn't be happy until she had wrecked Noelle Reynolds' life.

After she finished dressing, she called Billy. As

usual, he came running. She needed help with her "project."

When Billy arrived, she let him in and offered him a cup of coffee. Stella wondered if Billy's wife knew where he was right now.

"Sure, Stell, I'll take one. What's going on?"

"Do you remember loaning me your camera?"

"Yeah." Stella went on to explain everything to Billy—everything, as told through Stella's eyes.

"So this lady hired you to trick this guy, got you fired, and now she is married to him—all just so she could get him to sign a contract?"

"She is a naughty girl, and she needs to be punished, Billy."

"What do you need me to do, Stell?"

"I need to talk to John."

"How come you can't call him?"

"I'm sure he wouldn't take my call, and by now, he has changed the code on his gate."

"I need for you to act like you have a delivery for his house assistant, Maria."

"She will buzz you in, and I will be hiding in the back of your van."

"By the time I am finished, he will regret ever meeting Noelle Reynolds."

● ● ●

The sun came up and went down, and Noelle

had slept throughout the night, late into the next morning. She had missed work and hadn't called Jacqui. Jacqui probably hated her by now.

She had to get dressed. She made a decision. Her lease was up January 24, and she was moving. At one point, taming the big city had been thrilling, but it was too powerful. It had broken her. She was finished.

Noelle felt hollow inside. She was alone, and she had no one to blame but herself. Noelle had never experienced this kind of heartbreak. She had lost her pride, her future, and her heart.

She wasn't going to wait until her lease ended. She had already paid her rent so she could move whenever she pleased. She got dressed and called a moving company to bring boxes. While she waited, she picked up a few things and started working on getting organized.

Her brief spurts of work were laced with sudden outbursts of sobbing. She knew the right thing to do was to call Jacqui, but she couldn't talk to her without crying. She decided to leave without telling anyone. When she got to wherever she was going, she would call and let Jacqui know what happened. Jacqui was the kindest person she had ever met; maybe she would find it in her heart to forgive her.

The doorbell rang. Noelle assumed the boxes

had arrived so she opened the door without much thought.

Michael stood there silently.

● ● ●

Jacqui had determined that Noelle was not coming in, and she sent John on his way. She had decided to go to Noelle's apartment when she closed the office for the day.

She had done her best to cover for Noelle with the Board. When one member called, she informed him that Noelle had indeed been meeting with John Brittingham. The buzz that news created overshadowed the fact that Noelle hadn't been in the office for over a week. No one seemed concerned about Noelle, except Jacqui.

Jacqui struggled through things as well as she could. Several things needed Noelle's signature or approval. Authors were starting to get impatient and were asking some very tough questions.

She stayed late that night, trying to get caught up. She checked Noelle's voice mail and answered as many e-mails for her as she could. Some things had to be done, and she just had no choice but to do them to the best of her ability. They had gone through this when Roger died, and now it felt like a reccurring, bad dream.

● ● ●

John had given up for now. Noelle would have to calm down so he could reason with her. The trip back to his ranch was long and lonely. He had not been able to contact Noelle at all, and he had no idea where Stella actually lived. The hotel had never heard of her when he went to check with them.

John did what he usually did when he was upset; he worked. Some of his best writing took place when his feelings and emotions were running high. Over the last few years, he had become an emotional zombie, and he struggled at times in keeping true to the characters. He had to fight the urge to make the characters no more than what he knew his reading public wanted.

He settled in at his computer. There seemed to be a physical difference in the way he felt toward his steady love. He had neglected her, and now she seemed indifferent and cold. He started slowly and kept things simple. Before long, his fingers were flying over her, and he was telling her the secrets of his soul.

He hadn't written like this in years. He wept as he wrote the chapter where the protagonist broke up with his lover. He knew what true grief felt like for the first time ever, and he hated that he had taken it so lightly before in his other novels. He would never write the same way again.

John was so involved with his work that he

didn't hear Maria authorize a floral delivery. Maria asked the driver to pull to the back of the house. When the driver got out and came to the door, Maria didn't notice Stella sneaking out the side door of the van, going to the guesthouse. Once Billy left, he would wait just a little ways down the road from the gate, out of the camera's view.

As soon as he drove off and Maria went back inside, Stella crept in through the sunroom. She went past Maria, who was in the kitchen, without so much as a glance from Maria. John's office was down the hall, and knowing him, he was working. She got closer and closer to the door. She heard him clicking away on his keyboard. She stood outside of his door, trying to control her breathing. She could hear her heart beating in her ears.

She wasn't really afraid of anyone, but she needed a drink badly. Her hands were shaking, and she felt hot and a little dizzy. As bad as she felt, she knew there was no turning back now. She rounded the corner and stood in the doorway.

"Hello, John."

John looked up in shock. "How did you get in here?"

"Did you miss me?"

"Get out of here. Now." John reached for the phone to call the police.

"Not so fast, Romeo." Stella sounded serious,

and as if from nowhere, she pulled out a small, silver gun.

John sat the phone down. "What do you want from me?"

"I don't want anything from you. I just want what's mine."

"I don't understand."

"Where is that twit you married?"

"How did you know I got married?"

"Oh, John. I know everything. Haven't you figured that out by now?"

"Stella, tell me what you want."

"Where is Noelle?"

"Noelle doesn't live here anymore."

"Quit lying. I saw her moving in here."

"She did move in, but your little stunt ruined everything. She left me."

Stella laughed. With her hands already shaking, the gun was making John nervous. "Oh, that's too bad," Stella said mockingly.

"Stella, I want you to leave. Noelle is not here."

"Where is she?"

"I don't know. I haven't seen or spoken to her since she left."

"She owes me, and I want to see her."

"I told you. She won't have anything to do with me."

"Well, she will now. Let's go."

"Go where?"

"We're going to her apartment."

"I don't know where she lives," John lied.

"You're a liar, but it doesn't matter. I know where she lives. Now let's go."

"You'll never get past the security cameras."

"Oh, I think I will. You see, if I have any problems, Maria won't be able to go home to that little family she loves so much. You better make a believer out of Maria when you leave."

John watched her. She looked desperate, and desperate people did desperate things. He decided he should take her at her word this time.

"Let me call Maria on the intercom. We can leave out from the side door."

"I would be very, very careful if I were you."

"I understand." John picked up the phone. "Maria, I am going out for a while." John hung up and picked up his car keys. "Let's leave through here—just promise me you won't hurt Maria."

"You be a good boy, and Maria will never know I was here."

They got into the car parked at the side of the house. As John went out through the gate, he wondered if he would ever see Maria or his home again.

They drove a short distance, and Stella had him pull the car over. Billy was waiting inside the van. She kept the gun on John as he got out and climbed into the van.

"What are you doing, Stella?" Billy was shocked.

"I told you. Noelle Reynolds has to pay."

"Stell, I understand, but I never agreed to this. You just said you were going to talk to him. You've crossed the line, Stell."

"Shut up, Billy! Just shut up! I'm not like that mealy-mouthed, spineless woman you are married to. Noelle owes me, and she's going to pay. I can do this with or without you, but I would choose wisely." She dragged the gun across his stubbled jawline.

Stella held the gun on John as they road in silence to the penthouse. When they arrived, Stella told Billy that he could leave, which he gratefully did. Stella walked past Stan the doorman, right behind John.

"Good evening, Mr. Brittingham," Stan called out.

"Hello." John kept it short, hoping to draw as little attention as possible. They stepped into the elevator and rode to the top floor. All the way up, John tried to think of ways to stop Stella. If he wasn't careful, Stella would kill him. Then she would kill Noelle. He had to stay alive to protect her.

"Stella, whatever you want, I'll give it to you, just leave Noelle alone."

"Shut up, John."

Stella stood behind John as he approached Noelle's door. John hoped Noelle had the door locked. How could one bad choice have this many consequences?

Stella really needed a drink. It was going to be a long night.

All virtue is summed up in dealing justly.

ARISTOTLE

14

Noelle looked at Michael. He had changed some. Even though only two years had passed, he looked older, a little heavier, and tired.

"Michael. I don't know what to say."

"You could invite me in."

"Of course, come on in. What are you doing here?"

"Noelle, everything is a mess. I didn't know who else to turn to."

"I heard you were happy with your new wife."

"I was, eventually. Noelle, when you left me that day in September, I still loved you. I didn't want to live when you left me. You were everything I had ever wanted. I met my wife one night when I was at the bar. I was married to her on October 15. It hadn't even been a month. She was like Novocain for my heart."

"I knew you married her quickly, but I didn't know why."

"I'll admit that I married her for the wrong reasons, but after a time, I fell in love with her. It was the real kind of love that a husband should have for his wife."

"So what happened?"

"She left me."

"Why?"

"She was so jealous of you. She never believed that I had stopped loving you and that I loved only her. It didn't matter what I said. She started complaining to some guy she worked with. Before I knew it, she had the idea that there was something missing in her life."

"I'm sorry."

"Then I really messed up."

"What do you mean?"

"I have been waiting on her to come back, just trying to hang in there. The other night, though, I got tired of waiting. It was Christmas Eve, and I was lonely and feeling sorry for myself. I didn't know where my wife was spending Christmas, and I became discouraged. I just gave up on everything—my marriage, my family, my hope for a good future. Then I met this woman. She was beautiful, and I ended up taking her back to my condo."

"Who was she?"

"I don't know, and I don't know what happened." He went on to tell her about losing his money and probably any hope for reconciliation.

Noelle was doing her best to comfort him, but she was in bad shape herself. As they were sitting and talking, they heard a knock at the door.

Worlds were about to collide.

● ● ●

"I'm sorry Michael," Noelle apologized. "I ordered boxes from a moving company, and I guess they are here."

"I understand."

"Do you mind if I get the door?"

"No, of course not. I'm the one intruding."

"It will only take a minute, and you're not intruding." Noelle kept talking as she walked over to the door and turned to face her visitor.

"I'm here with the boxes, Ms. Reynolds." The mover had his arms full.

"That's wonderful. Please, just bring them in and set them in the dining room."

"Noelle, do you mind if I get some water?" Michael asked.

"Help yourself. Kitchen is to the left."

"I've got a few more boxes in the hall." The mover stepped back through Noelle's front door and brought the last group in.

"That should do it," the mover said.

"Thank you." Noelle stepped to the door as he left. As she closed the door behind him, she felt the door push open.

John came through the door, pushed in by Stella. "What are you doing here?" Noelle asked in shock.

"Noelle, she has a gun," said John.

Noelle stood still, not moving. Stella glared at her. "Sit on the sofa and shut up," Stella ordered Noelle. Noelle went to the sofa and sat down. "Get over there by her," she motioned to John.

He slid over next to Noelle and tried to take her hand. She jerked it back, scooting as far away from him as she could.

"Noelle, I'm so sorry. Please let me . . ." John tried to make amends.

"Shut up! I don't want to hear about your little love spat." Stella was irritated and physically trembling.

"Hey, Noelle, do you mind if I make some coffee?" Michael turned the corner and saw Stella.

"What are you doing here?"

Stella couldn't contain the shock on her face at seeing Mike. "You've got to be kidding me."

"Stella. Everyone had better hold onto your wallet. Miss Stella has sticky fingers."

John looked at Michael. "It's you."

"What are you doing with her?" Michael asked John, while watching Stella.

"You know her?" John asked.

"Remember when I said I met a woman who took me home and stole my money? Meet Stella."

"What are you doing here, Mike?" John asked.

"You know the story I told you about the woman I almost married?"

"Yes."

"That woman was Noelle."

John physically tensed up. He looked at the picture on the fireplace. Now he knew why Mike looked so familiar that night in the bar. He fixed his eyes on Noelle, and the hurt flooded across his face. Noelle wanted to tell him that it was a misunderstanding, but she couldn't. Part of her felt bad, but part of her didn't care. She might not have been upfront with him, but he had out-and-out lied.

"Isn't this cozy?" Stella said sarcastically. "You get on the sofa with them." She used the gun to motion Michael over to the sofa. "All of you shut up and listen to me. I could care less about any of you losers. I just want what is mine," Stella said.

"I don't understand why you are here," Noelle said.

"Come on, Noelle. I'm not stupid like your little business deal sitting next to you." Noelle hung her head.

Even John didn't deserve this.

● ● ●

Jacqui finished her long day and asked the company driver to take her to Noelle's penthouse. Before she left, she checked the machine one more time. There was a message from John Brittingham, still looking for Noelle. Maybe she would have something to tell him tomorrow.

When she got to Noelle's building, she bumped into Stan. She had spoken to him all the times she had visited Noelle throughout the last year or so. She asked him if he had seen Noelle.

"You know, I haven't actually seen her since Christmas Day."

"You saw her on Christmas?"

"Sure. She and her new husband were just here long enough for her to grab a few things."

"Her new husband?"

"Oh, I thought you knew, since you work together. Maybe I shouldn't have said anything."

"Stan, I haven't seen her or spoken to her. She should have been back at work two days ago. Would you mind if I went upstairs to check on her?"

"No problem. I saw her husband going that way earlier, only..."

"Only what?"

"There was this other woman with him. Now don't take this wrong, but she was an attractive woman. He wasn't flirting with her or anything. He kind of even acted like he was agitated with her."

"So you think he is in the penthouse with another woman?"

"Unless I didn't see him leave."

"I'm going to go on up."

"Let me know if I can help," Stan offered.

"Stan, if I don't come back down within an hour, will you come and check on me?"

"Do you want me to go up with you?" Stan asked.

"No, that's okay. I just hope she's home."

Jacqui went up to the penthouse, stopping to listen through the door before she knocked. She could hear shouting and angry voices. She thought about what she should do, and she decided to knock anyway.

The conversation in the penthouse stopped when they realized someone was at the door. Stella signaled for everyone to be quiet. They all waited to see what would happen next, hoping help was on the other side.

Stella kept the gun facing the sofa, but walked

to the peephole to look out. She didn't recognize the woman on the other side. The woman at the door knocked again.

There was nothing but whispers for the next few minutes. Something made Jacqui feel afraid, and she immediately started praying. She prayed for safety, and she prayed for discernment.

"I know you are in there," Jacqui shouted.

Noelle recognized Jacqui's voice immediately. She really hoped Stella would let Jacqui walk off.

"I can't let her call the police," Stella said. "Go let her in." Noelle walked toward the door. *Please turn around and leave Jacqui!* Noelle wished she could will Jacqui to leave, but she knew that wasn't going to happen.

Jacqui heard the lock click on the door and saw the knob starting to turn. Somebody was not anxious to see her.

"Hi, Jacqui." Noelle hesitantly greeted Jacqui as she opened the door.

"Noelle, are you all right?"

Noelle tried to move her eyes to signal to Jacqui that there was a problem. Jacqui just acted confused and kept talking.

"I'm really fine. May I give you a call in the morning?" Noelle's speech sounded formal and stilted. Jacqui knew that something was not right. Noelle heard Stella clear her throat.

"Jacqui, please come in. I am so sorry."

"About what?" As Jacqui stepped through the door, she understood the seriousness of the situation.

"Both of you sit down. Who is this?"

"My assistant," Noelle said.

"I see. Your assistant. That figures. You are a busy girl. I guess you need an assistant. How long have you worked for the princess?" Stella asked, looking at Jacqui. Jacqui didn't answer.

"I asked you a question. How long have you worked for her?"

"A few years, I guess."

"Well, this is one mess you won't be able to help her Royal Highness out of."

"What do you want from me?" Noelle asked.

"I haven't had any work since you got me fired."

"How did I get you fired?" Noelle honestly had no idea what this crazy woman was talking about.

"You are a liar! You know you told Molly Red I was moving too slowly, and she fired me."

"You're the woman who worked with Molly Red?"

"Don't act like you don't know. You aren't as stupid as you look."

"She never told me who you were. She just said

she hadn't heard from you since the second day on the case."

"How convenient for you. Why couldn't you leave me alone? I would have got your precious contract signed, but no. You couldn't wait."

"Stella, I never told her that you were too slow. I said nothing seemed to be working, and I was out of time. I had to take matters into my own hands."

Noelle hated to word it that way; John was bound to take all of this the wrong way. She wondered what he was thinking about everything he was hearing. It was obvious that the reality of Michael being in her home had crushed him. As angry she was with him, she didn't want him to find out about the private investigator or Michael like this.

"You've had everything handed to you on a silver platter. I've always had to make my own way. When John came along, I saw an opportunity to have what I wanted in life. I would be the one who everyone wanted to be with, the one who could buy whatever I wanted."

"What do you want from me now, Stella?"

"Somebody is going to pay for all of this misery. I want money and lots of it."

"Stella, I don't have any money." Noelle answered truthfully.

"I can tell." Stella looked around the noticeably expensive penthouse.

"Stella, I am maxed to the hilt on credit cards, and I don't have any money in savings. I am letting my apartment go on January 24." She wished she didn't have to share everything with everyone under these circumstances, but Stella needed to know she was telling the truth.

"Although none of this surprises me, I know you have more money. You are married to John Brittingham."

Jacqui and Michael both turned to look at John and Noelle. "Not anymore." Noelle looked at John.

"How much money do you want?" John asked.

"$250,000."

"I'll pay it," John said.

"John, you don't owe me anything." Noelle hated being obligated to him.

"You're right; I don't. You were also right when you said we aren't married. However, I want to get out of here alive. Stella, go with me to the bank, and I'll get you the money."

"What would I do with the rest of them? They would have the police on me before we ever got there."

"Then what do you want me to do?"

"I want you to call the bank and have the money transferred to my account."

"I can't get that kind of money over the phone."

"Stop lying. You need to remember something, Sweetie. I don't care that your 'wife' spent thousands of dollars stalking you, just to get you to sign a contract. I don't care if Mike, sitting here, hooks up with your wife or his own wife. I don't even care if Noelle stays married to you or not. In fact, I don't care if I kill you all. I only care about the money. So make it happen."

"Please, John. She will kill us anyway. The minute you transfer the money, we're dead," Noelle said.

"Don't you trust me, Noelle?" Stella laughed, breaking into a smoker's cough.

"Stella, let everyone else go. I'll stay," said Noelle.

"You don't have any money. Remember?" Stella was getting agitated. "Get the bank called." Stella looked at John, and she was all business.

John stood up slowly to go to the phone. As he walked past Stella, she turned to watch him. Just as her eyes shifted to him, Jacqui jumped up and threw herself toward Stella. Stella swung her shaky arm around and fired the gun.

Before Jacqui could reach her, John turned, placing himself between Jacqui and Stella. He fell to the floor as the bullet struck his chest.

Stella lost her balance and fell backward, hitting her head on the fireplace. She lay there unconscious.

UNHINGED

Noelle rushed to John. "John! John!" She tried to see if he was breathing. He looked very pale and his breathing was shallow. "Hold on! Don't die on me!"

Michael asked if Noelle and Jacqui were okay and hurriedly called 911. "My ankle is hurt. It might be broken," Jacqui answered. "How's John?"

"He's bleeding badly, Jacqui," Noelle replied.

"The ambulance is on its way," Michael said, as he hung up the phone.

"Michael, grab me some towels out of the hall closet. I need to try and stop this bleeding," Noelle said.

Michael brought back the towels, and Noelle applied pressure to John's chest. Jacqui tried to stand, but she couldn't. She looked over at Stella. "Is she alive?"

"I don't know, and honestly, I don't care," Noelle replied.

Jacqui took a towel and crawled over to Stella. Stella looked like she was still breathing.

"How can you do that?" Noelle asked.

"Because it is the right thing to do," Jacqui answered, while placing the towel under Stella's head.

"How can you say that? She tried to kill you." Noelle's eyes and voice snapped at Jacqui.

Jacqui stayed calm and looked kindly at Noelle.

"So we only have to minister to the hurting or wounded if we like them? If they're nice?" Jacqui was trying to feel a pulse in Stella's arm.

"Of course not."

"So what's the difference?" Jacqui asked Noelle.

"There is a difference between 'not nice' and a murderer," Noelle pointed out, while stroking John's face.

"Is there?" Noelle looked at her in disbelief. "According to whom?" Jacqui asked, while trying to move her leg to a more comfortable position.

"Jacqui, it's a basic fact of life. Everyone knows it."

"What does God know about it?" Jacqui's eyes met Noelle's.

"What are you asking? God says that we aren't supposed to kill other people, doesn't He?"

"When Jesus laid down his life, Noelle, did He do it for everyone or just for those with minor offenses?" Noelle hung her head down, looking at John.

Within just a few seconds, the ambulance arrived. The paramedics worked diligently on John.

"How bad is he?" Noelle asked the woman working on him.

"He is very unstable," she answered. "We need to get him to the hospital as quickly as possible.

The sooner we get him there, the better chance he'll have."

As they were loading John into an ambulance, the police came in to question Noelle. "What's going on here?" the officer asked her.

"This woman has been stalking my husband and me to extort money from us."

As the police continued to question the other three, a second ambulance came in to get Stella, and she was intentionally taken to a different hospital than John.

"Would it be possible to finish your questioning at the hospital?" Noelle asked.

"That will be fine, but the crime scene investigator will need to stay here," the officer told her.

"No problem. I would like to be with my husband, and she needs to get her ankle looked at." Noelle motioned toward Jacqui.

"Michael, I've got to go." Noelle looked at Michael with an apologetic look.

"Me too, but this time I really have to leave you, Noelle." She knew what he meant. She would never see Michael again.

The police stayed and looked at the evidence, taking several pictures and samples. Michael went home, hoping he could rebuild what he almost lost.

Noelle and Jacqui went to the hospital. Both were broken, only in different places.

• • •

As they arrived at the hospital, the press was everywhere. *How did they learn about this so quickly?* Noelle thought to herself.

The police escorted them into a family waiting room that the hospital had set up for them.

Once the door shut behind them, they tried to get things sorted out.

"How is my husband?" Noelle asked anxiously.

"He is still alive. However, he is in critical condition. The bullet nicked his heart," a hospital spokesman told her.

"When will you know something?"

"It could be several days before he is out of the woods, Mrs. Brittingham." The man didn't have a hopeful look on his face.

"When can I see him?" she asked.

"He is in surgery now. It will be five or six hours. Now what about you?" he asked, looking at Jacqui.

"I think it's broken," she replied.

"Well, if it is okay with the police, we'll get you down to x-ray."

"That will work. I need to take separate statements anyway," the officer said.

The hospital representative took Jacqui by wheelchair to get her ankle treated. Noelle really hoped Jacqui would not need surgery. She needed her by her side. This was too much to bear on her own.

"May I get you a glass of water before we start?" the officer asked her.

"That would be wonderful. My throat is so dry. I haven't had anything to drink since before Stella arrived at the penthouse."

"I'll be right back." When the officer returned, he asked Noelle to tell him the story from the beginning.

Noelle proceeded to tell him everything. It was almost like therapy for her. She hadn't been able to tell anyone, not even Jacqui. Things had happened too quickly.

After the officer was finished with her, he told her she could be excused. Noelle immediately went to check on her husband's status.

"He is still in surgery," the nurse at the station told her.

"What about my friend?"

"She should be through in x-ray. I'll take you to her."

Noelle followed the nurse down to one of the emergency patient rooms. Jacqui was sitting on the bed.

"Hi. How are you feeling?" Noelle asked.

"I feel pretty good, but my ankle is bad. The

doctor said that I need surgery. They are going to try to do the surgery in about four hours."

"Oh, Jacqui. I'm so sorry. What can I do to help?"

"Noelle, you've got so much on your mind. I'll be fine. You might want to call someone at work tomorrow."

"I'll do it. How could I have messed up this badly, Jacqui?"

"Oh, Honey. It wasn't a mess up. It was an opportunity for God to show you how big He is and how much He loves you."

"Jacqui, I wish I could believe, especially now. If God loves me so much, will He save John?"

"Sweetie, God is good all the time, no matter what happens with John. God will hold your heart while you walk through this valley, if you will let Him. Remember, Noelle, you have to surrender to Him. You have to come to the end of yourself."

"Jacqui, I promise that I'll think some more about it. Will you promise to get some rest before they operate?"

"I am feeling so tired. I just want to close my eyes for a minute." Noelle gave Jacqui a hug and told her she would be waiting outside in the family room if she needed her. The press had made it impossible for her to wait in the general waiting area.

Noelle turned out the light, left the room, and Jacqui closed her eyes for the last time that night.

• • •

Stella was in the emergency room, under police guard. She had regained consciousness, but she wasn't talking to anyone. She had suffered a mild concussion, but the police were still being allowed to question her.

"Ms. Stone, would you like to have an attorney present during questioning?" the officer asked.

Stella looked at him with her dead eyes. All she could think about was how badly she needed a drink.

*Every man has his secret sorrows
which the world knows not;
and often times we call a man cold
when he is only sad.*

HENRY WADSWORTH LONGFELLOW

15

Noelle went into the family room and sat down. Time seemed to move backward. Jacqui would be going into surgery almost as John was coming out. Noelle just couldn't take sitting still. She slipped down the stairs for a few minutes, just to gather her thoughts.

Noelle thought about calling her aunt, but she would be scared to death when she heard what had happened. Aunt Treena was a rock, but Noelle had created this mess, and she didn't want to pull her into it.

Noelle made it down to the third floor where she was able to sit for a little over an hour. However, it wasn't long before the press caught up with her. It was no use. They weren't going to let her suffer privately. She pleaded with them just to give her a brief moment alone, but they wouldn't listen to her.

Then the strangest thing happened. A calmness descended over the situation. She spoke clearly, asking them to step back, and they did. She climbed the stairs, went back into the family room, and didn't move. She sat there with no sounds other than hospital announcements coming over the speakers, penetrating through the door.

She thought about the night at The Westminster. It was a glamorous, wonderful, magical night. John was handsome, and she had cleaned up pretty well herself.

Who would have ever thought that night that she would be married to John? They had a great time in Vegas, and her hopes had been high. Now John might die, and she knew their marriage was ruined. She only wanted an opportunity to clear up the situation. After everything that had happened, she knew there was probably something more to the film Stella left at the door. Undoubtedly, Stella had set the entire situation up. Noelle wished she had believed John when he had tried to tell her.

She waited an hour or so, and then she decided to go check on Jacqui again. When she went into the room, her bed was empty. Noelle stepped back out to the nurses' station again.

UNHINGED

"Excuse me. Did they take my friend to surgery earlier than they anticipated?"

The nurse physically dropped her shoulders and tilted her head, as if she had bad news. "I'm so sorry. We looked for you, but you weren't in the family room when we went to find you. We thought you had gone home for a while."

"What the matter? Where's Jacqui?"

"Let's step back into the family room."

"Let's not. Where's Jacqui? Tell me now."

"Jacqui had a serious break. Sometimes a break like that can cause blood clots. We gave her an anticoagulant when we first treated her, but it was too late. The blood clot traveled to her heart. We lost her."

"No. No!" Noelle began sobbing and sunk down on the floor in a ball. She started hyperventilating, and then she passed out. The nurse immediately started checking her and working on her. Then the nurse had her moved to a private room.

Noelle was completely alone.

● ● ●

The lights from the machines glowed in the dark. It took Noelle's eyes time to adjust. As she looked around the room, she saw a clock that said 12:17. She must have passed out. Then she remembered what the nurse said about Jacqui.

Noelle didn't think she could cope with everything. Jacqui was dead, and John might be dead too. *If God is so good, why is this happening to me?* Noelle asked herself.

It was odd. In the calm silence of the night, Noelle had time to think. Jacqui loved her God, and she truly believed his plan was always perfect. Noelle wasn't sure she understood, but she knew that Jacqui had understood.

Over the last few days, she had been down as low as she thought she could go. She had been wrong.

Noelle lay there in the dim light. Jacqui had wanted her to know how much God loved her. She remembered the conversation she had with Jacqui over lunch. She desperately needed the kind of love Jacqui said only He could give. She needed to know there was Someone who would never leave her nor forsake her.

Jacqui said praying was just talking to God so Noelle closed her eyes. He was all she had left.

"God, I have always believed that You exist, but Jacqui said I need to have You in my heart. I need to know You, God. I've tried to be good, but I don't guess I gave much thought to what You wanted me to do. I did everything on my own, and now everything is screwed up. Please forgive me, God. I'm so sorry. I want to put You on the throne of my heart like Jacqui said. I am willing to give up having my way. I've always thought I could take care of myself, and I have failed. I want to put my faith in what Jesus did for me instead of myself.

"Jacqui always made sure I knew that Jesus died for me, for my sins. She said He would have died for me if I were the only person on the earth. I want to thank you for sending Him to pay the debt that I owe. Please God, let Jesus come into my heart. Forgive me.

"And God, I know Jacqui is with You. She knew You as I want to know You. So if it is possible, will you let Jacqui know that I asked Jesus to come and live in my heart? Please let John be okay. I want to make things right with him. Thanks."

Noelle did her best to remember everything Jacqui had told her in the past, but she wasn't sure she had. However, she knew she had prayed it with all of her heart, and Jacqui said that was what was important. For the first time in her life, she felt a sense of peace.

She got out of bed and went to check on John. He had made it out of surgery, but was in intensive care.

Noelle would not be allowed in for two more hours. The nurse said she would wake her as soon as it was possible for her to see him.

Noelle went back to her bed. It was the best two hours of sleep she had in months.

● ● ●

John peeked out through the slits in his eyes. *What happened?* he asked himself. He wasn't even sure where he was. It looked like a hospital. His chest felt heavy, as if it had pressure on it.

The memory was fuzzy at first, but then John was able to remember Stella being at Noelle's penthouse. He was here by himself. *Is everyone dead?* he wondered.

He tried to think of what had happened to each person, but he couldn't. *Wouldn't Noelle be here if she were okay?* John wondered.

Within a few minutes, a nurse came in to check on him. She changed the IV bag and checked his vitals.

"Have you seen my wife?"

"I think she was admitted."

"Admitted? What's wrong with her?"

"Mostly stress, I think. She should be down here shortly."

"Thank you."

John didn't know what he would say to Noelle when she came in. She was probably still angry with him, but he was desperate to talk to her. Even though she hadn't told him the truth about everything, all of this just wasn't worth it. After all, the way they started out was scary and probably not very smart.

John wanted to see her. He wanted her to come home.

• • •

"Mrs. Brittingham, you may go see your husband now."

"Thank you." Noelle sat up. She was completely exhausted, but she felt good. Even with everything that had happened, she felt hopeful. Maybe John would want to hear what had happened to her. It might actually help his heart to feel as good as hers did.

Noelle tried to clean up. The clothes she had worn earlier were covered in John's blood. The nurse offered to bring her a set of scrubs, and she gladly changed from her hospital gown into the clean outfit. It wasn't fancy, but it was comfortable and ready to go.

She walked into his room and watched him as he slept. All of their troubles were small compared to seeing him hooked up to the monitors and the IV. He looked pale.

She pulled the chair closer to his bed. The only sound in the room was the pumping and clicking of the machines as they monitored his progress. She bowed her head and prayed for God to take care of him. She asked God to give her a second chance, and she thanked God for the gift He had given her in her hospital bed.

As Noelle prayed, with her head bowed, John opened his eyes and saw her. He thought she had never looked as beautiful as she did praying. Without speaking, he slid his fingers into her hand as it rested beside him.

She looked up, with tear-filled eyes, and said, "Oh, John. You're awake! Are you okay? I'm so sorry. I have to tell..."

"Shh, not now. Let's just be together. I love you, Noelle."

"I love you too."

They held hands in the stillness of the room, with the rest of the world hustling around right outside of their door. Of all the things they had done and of all the places they had been, this was the most romantic moment they had shared.

Their hearts were truly one.

● ● ●

Several days passed, and John started feeling better. Noelle had stayed by his side, except to attend Jacqui's funeral. Noelle had decided not to return to work at the publishing house. John was encouraging her to write the novel that she had always dreamed about, and she was looking forward to a new life with a fresh start.

When John felt up to it, the police came back, talked to John, asked Noelle a few more questions, and updated them on everything. Stella was out of the hospital, but she had been taken to the county jail, where she was awaiting her hearing. Noelle thought the news would make her feel relieved, but instead she had a kind of sad feeling.

What kept her from being like Stella? She had thought a lot about that lately. Stella seemed evil, but she didn't know the Lord.

She thought about the question Jacqui had asked her that day. If she were to stand in front of God, and He were to ask why He should let her into his Heaven, what would she say? Now that she had asked Jesus into her heart, she understood what the answer had to be. She knew Jesus personally, and she had given her heart to God.

She wondered how Stella would answer the question. Had anyone ever asked her? What if Stella never had a Jacqui in her life, someone who cared enough to make sure she knew Jesus. Thinking about Stella left her with very mixed emotions. Stella wasn't good, but neither was Noelle. Noelle still sinned, and she knew it. She knew the day would come when she would have to give Stella the same opportunity that she had been given.

As she pondered these things, she couldn't help but think of John. They had never talked much about spiritual things, except for that night at her aunt's house. How would John answer Jacqui's question?

John and Noelle had many hours to talk about their misunderstandings. Everything was worked out, and Noelle understood that Stella intentionally made the tape look bad. John understood that Noelle really did not love Michael, because she never understood what love was, until now.

Before too long, John was released to go home. Their hearts ached to make a fresh start. They made the long drive into the country and pulled up in front of their home. Noelle helped John toward the door. She looked at the step that had held the terrible Christmas gift.

She didn't want to say anything negative to ruin the moment, but she prayed silently that God would help her forget. As immediately as she prayed, God answered her. She knew at once that she was never to forget that gift, for by receiving that wretched gift, wrapped in hate, she had found her way to a gift that was perfect, true, and faithful. She had received the gift of eternal life. Just as the bad gift was exchanged for the good one, Jesus had exchanged his life for hers.

As John stepped onto the porch, he said, "Looking at this step brings back bad memories."

Noelle smiled. "You know, John, we never

exchanged gifts on Christmas, and I think it is time."

"I don't have anything for you, Noelle. We can't do the exchange now."

"John, everything you need is only a prayer away. When we get you settled, I want to talk to you about exchanging that bad gift we were given with the most perfect gift ever." John had no idea what she was talking about, but he loved her and trusted her.

As they entered through their doorway, they began their eternity together.

Note from the author ...

I did not become a Christian until I was 30 years old. That's a lot of time to disobey God.

Yet in his grace, He allowed me to be adopted into his family simply by accepting the free gift of salvation made possible only through Christ.

My prayer for you, the reader, is that you would see how much God loves you, no matter where you are in life.

There is no one too bad or too far over the line to become a member of God's family.

I should know.

Maybe there is a little bit of Stella in all of us if we are truthful, and Stella needs a heart change.

Cover Designer Sommer Buss

Home videos of Sommer Buss as a little girl with the important things in life—pink curlers in her hair, Miss Piggy clothing, and a pencil in hand—are proof that she was born to be an artist. There wasn't a time when she wasn't drawing or scribbling on something. At the age of nine, while touring the animation department at MGM Studios in Disney World, she realized that she, too, could create beautiful artwork for a living.

Sommer graduated with Distinction from the University of Oklahoma in 2002, majoring in visual communications and minoring in art history. She is currently the Director of Creative Design for Tate Publishing and Enterprises, LLC where she designs book covers, ads, and catalogs as well as oversees the entire graphic design staff.

Sommer says the following about her career, "I love what I do and I'm passionate about design. However, more than that, I love that my job is about more than design alone—I have a part in changing the world for Christ."

Layout Designer
Kristen Polson

From as far back as she can remember, amidst dreams of being a movie star, mother, and pitcher for the Cubs, Kristen Polson has always been drawn to expressing life through the visual arts. She currently works as a graphic design artist at Tate Publishing and Enterprises, LLC, where she creates book covers, text layout, and illustrations.

She also enjoys working on her more traditional fine art—especially oil painting and graphic photography. She has exhibited her work recently in a show called "Eclectricity" with colleague Sommer Buss in Yukon, OK. She has also shown her work in the Davis Hall Gallery, 3rd Floor Gallery, and Studio Theatre in Chickasha, OK.

Kristen graduated with honors from the University of Science and Arts of Oklahoma in 2004 where she majored in art and minored in musical theatre.

She is currently in the process of moving to southern California with her husband.

Please visit her Web site at kdpgraphics.com

Shaken, Not Stirred

Ever find yourself searching for answers when someone asks what the Bible says about the believer and alcohol?

Finally, there is help! Dan Fisher's book *Shaken, Not Stirred* takes a hard, no nonsense, biblical look at drinking. This author draws a line in the sand and dares the reader to choose sides. If you want to know the *truth* about the Bible, the believer, and the bottle, this book is for you!

I have known Dan for years, and I praise God for him and his book! In it, he takes a totally honest look historically, philosophically, and most importantly, biblically, at what the Christian's response to alcohol should be. God has used this study to lead me to a clear decision on how I will respond to drinking for the rest of my life. Every Christian should read this book—it will seriously challenge and bless you.

Joel Engle
Worship Leader &
Recording Artist for Doxology Records

Order your copy today!

Shaken, Not Stirred

Tate Publishing, LLC at
www.tatepublishing.com
888.361.9473

Contact author Stacy Baker
at stacy@tatepublishing.com

or order more copies of this book at

TATE PUBLISHING, LLC

127 East Trade Center Terrace
Mustang, Oklahoma 73064

(888) 361 - 9473

Tate Publishing, LLC

www.tatepublishing.com